Death Comes Up Short

Outside the Circle Mystery, Volume 5

Shereen Vedam

Published by Shereen Vedam, 2023.

This is a work of fiction. Similarities to real people, places, or events are entirely coincidental.

DEATH COMES UP SHORT

First edition. July 11, 2023.

ISBN: 978-1989036198

Written by Shereen Vedam.

This book is dedicated to Enid Blyton for coaching me on how to have fun as a child.

Chapter One

"Abbie, River is over there." Jimi waved madly at a young boy his age at the far end of the school's car park.

The day was bright under a beautiful blue sky with the air scented by a fresh-cut lawn. A scattering of people who had left the school car park earlier now climbed toward the school's front doors. Above those doors, a gigantic violet banner with white lettering welcomed visitors with, "Congratulations!"

The school had invited parents, caretakers, and guardians, like Abbie, for a celebration. They'd set up games for the kids in the field out back, and tours and seminars for the adults inside.

"Can I go?" Jimi bounced and pointed to his friend. At seven years of age, Jimi was growing up to be an independent thinker who was a handful to manage.

River Spencer Irvine and Jimi had become fast friends this past term. She hadn't met River before she heard about the boy's burgeoning friendship. Once she saw River, recognition was instant. This short, brown-haired, freckled boy was the same one the goddess Kali had shown Abbie in a photo last autumn.

Ever since, Abbie had been wondering about him. Was he someone to be protected? Or someone to beware?

While she waited to see if Jimi's new friendship was here to stay, Abbie and her friends checked into the Irvines' background.

River's parents had recently moved their family from the southern tip of Cornwall to Chipstead, Kent. The father had gained a dive instructor position at the local leisure center.

River's mother was a therapist specializing in counseling psychology.

Abbie then engineered an introduction with River's family. During that meeting, the parents presented themselves as perfectly "normal," with a British mother and Irish father.

As the term progressed, Abbie never let down her guard around the boy, waiting for the other shoe to drop. Especially as River and Jimi quickly grew into BFFs.

She now knelt to be at eye level with Jimi and waited until his distracted gaze met hers. "You two are to keep your masks on at all times, understand? This pandemic isn't over."

"Yes," Jimi said, his attention swerving to his friend.

"And no supe talk," she added for good measure.

For the first time, Jimi hesitated. He gazed at her with concern over the edge of his blue King Arthur mask before his attention swung back to his friend. River, of a similar height to Jimi, waved widely. He had on a black hoodie, dark trousers, and a smiling-toothy mask.

"Even with another supe?" Jimi asked.

Before the first day back at school, Abbie had "the talk" with Jimi. No talking about supernatural abilities or events to anyone other than Standard Bearer club members. Abbie's SB group investigated supernatural calamities. So far, he'd been good at keeping to that promise. Until now.

"What other supe?" she asked, worried.

"I can't tell you," Jimi replied solemnly. "We pinkie squirted about it."

Abbie glanced at Nica, wondering if she had any sibling insights about this odd ritual. The girl shrugged to say she had no clue what her brother was talking about.

"What is a pinkie squirt?" Abbie asked.

"Like this." Jimi wrapped his pinkie around Abbie's and held them up, grinning. "Only when I do that with River, he can make water squirt up. Then we swore we wouldn't tell anyone else about our supe talks."

She couldn't fathom this water squirting up thing. Was it something Jimi had done, asking for water nearby to come and bless their pact? Or could River manipulate water?

"Jimi, is River a supe?" Abbie asked, point blank.

Jimi slammed his hand across his masked mouth, his eyes squinting mischievously. No talking, they'd pinkie squirted. Understood.

She assumed this also meant Jimi had confided in his new BFF about his ability to talk to any object. Abbie released a resigned sigh. What could she do about it now? At least the boys had sworn to keep their chit-chat between themselves.

She lifted Jimi's chin until he met her gaze again. "No going off of school grounds without my permission."

"I won't," Jimi said. "I promise."

"All right." Abbie released his chin and extended her arms to hug him and inhale his lovely scent of strawberry jam on toast—his two favorite food groups. Too soon, he was off, racing toward his friend, leaving her outstretched arms empty.

She wished Robert had been here with her. Then she could have sent the ghost to follow Jimi and make sure he wouldn't get into trouble. But today was one of those rare times since she met Robert, who had died in 1816, that he was not with her. He was in St. Michael's graveyard beside his daughter's grave. It was the anniversary of her death.

To give Robert the privacy he needed to grieve his

daughter's passing, Abbie came alone to this school party. They were here to applaud all the children moving up a level. It didn't matter how much or little they'd learned while being home-schooled because of last year's COVID lockdown.

Nica then tugged at Abbie's sleeve, wanting to go chat to her classmates.

Something inside her screamed, *I'm not ready to let you go, too.*

At the ten-year-old's confused look, Abbie sighed and nodded, then immediately felt bereft as Nica ran off.

Abbie entered the school alone and strolled through the halls, reading notices on billboards and checking in on the various seminars.

Within a half-hour, she tip-toed out of an informational talk on "Understanding the lingering risks of COVID-19" and headed out to the field. To her left, boys ran around, chasing each other with dandelion plants and shouting, "pee the bed." The sight brought back memories of her three elder brothers playing that same game when they were all kids.

Nica kicked a ball around with her football friends. Straight ahead, the year-three kids were involved in a serious egg-and-spoon race. Jimi and River stood side-by-side, giving each other sneaky looks and whispering to their eggs balanced on spoons.

Suspecting they were up to no good, she sent a message through Hafgufa. Using her magical Grimm cord embedded within her right arm, she telepathically warned Jimi. *"No cheating!"*

She wanted to ensure he wasn't about to talk his and River's eggs into staying on their spoons.

"Aw, Abbie," he responded in a put-upon manner.

"Unless you two believe you're incapable of winning this race fairly?"

Jimi's shoulders dropped, signaling she'd won this argument. River gave her a nasty look and Abbie folded her arms and returned the stare. Jimi tugged at his friend's sleeve until he looked away with a scowl.

In the end, River won the race, with Jimi coming in a close second. The boys' loud whoops and jumping proclaimed their supreme satisfaction with their performance. Abbie was well pleased because, to be that joyful, they must have placed well by effort and determination alone.

They ran to collect their reward—two helium balloons. The balloons were brighter and flashier than the ones the other children received for participation.

A well-built young man—close to Abbie in age—strolled to chat up the two boys. He looked familiar, but she couldn't immediately place him. Abbie asked the woman beside her if she recognized the fellow.

"Oh, that's Shane Irvine," the woman said. "Isn't he gorgeous?"

Of course. Shane Irvine was River's uncle. A star athlete and an Olympic hopeful. Abbie had never met him, but she'd seen his photo on social media and during the research her friends helped her do on River's family.

"Sad about what happened to him earlier this summer," the woman beside her continued.

Abbie had gathered her information months ago. She couldn't recall hearing any recent news about Shane Irvine, so she asked, "What happened?"

"After he tested positive for COVID, he missed the cutoff to join the Summer Olympics team."

Abbie's gaze swung toward the diver with concern, and she was about to sprint up and tug her child away. What was he doing socializing? "Shouldn't he be isolating?"

"He recovered quickly, but it was too late to attend the games. He was heartbroken."

Abbie nodded, her sympathy rising. The Olympics only came around once every four years.

"It was a tragedy or a victory," the woman continued with a twisted smile, "depending on your outlook."

"What do you mean?" Abbie asked.

"We still brought home the gold for the ten-meter platform, love. If he'd gone," she shrugged, "who knows? We might have had to settle for a third bronze instead." She winked at Abbie. "Irvine's good, but he's no Daley."

Abbie recognized the name Daley. He was a recent favorite in Britain after bringing home the gold at the Summer Olympics.

She glanced back at the field and noticed Jimi, River, and Shane Irvine were no longer there. She scanned, looking for her boy. Spotting Nica, she waved.

"What's up, Abbie?" Nica asked, running to her.

"Do you know where your brother's gone?" Abbie asked, already contacting her Grimm cord. *"Find Jimi."*

"What's up, Abbie?" Jimi responded instantly.

Abbie's breath gushed out in relief.

Nica tilted her head as if she, too, had heard his response. "Where are you, little nightmare?"

"Don't call me that," Jimi answered, sounding put-out. *"I*

haven't had a nightmare in months. I'm with River and his uncle. We're walking to their car. River's Uncle Shane has to return home right away."

"Stop where you are and wait for us," Abbie said. Her panic lowered, but didn't die. "We'll be right there."

"I didn't leave the school grounds, Abbie," he said, sounding confused.

"You did well."

She and Nica raced in silence toward the back door of the school. It would be a shorter route to the front if they cut through school corridors.

"River wants me to come over for a sleepover. Is that okay, Abbie?"

"No," Abbie said, her panic returning. "Jimi, and tell River to stay with you."

There was a moment of silence and then Jimi said, *"River can't stay. His Uncle Shane says he's in a hurry and has to leave now."*

Abbie and Nica had reached the front doors and were racing down the steps before Jimi finished speaking. They arrived by his side panting, to find him all alone, holding his and River's balloons.

Once she caught her breath, Abbie said, "Which way?"

Jimi pointed straight ahead to the car park. Shane Irvine was getting into a gold Nissan Leaf. She and her kids sprinted up to it, but the car sped away in a screech of tires before they reached it. Seriously suspicious.

"Are we going to chase after them?" Nica asked, excited, as if she had scented an adventure.

"Yes!" Jimi shouted, jumping up and down.

"No," Abbie said, speed-dialing Judith, a police officer and member of the SB club. "We don't know yet if River's in trouble."

Was she overreacting because Kali had shown her that image of River? After all, Shane Irvine was his uncle.

"Who's there?" Judith asked, sounding sensual.

Abbie cringed. She'd forgotten it was risky calling Judith on her days off. Now that she and Bran were dating, who knew what state her friend would be in on a Saturday morning? Abbie quickly explained what had happened and asked for Judith's professional viewpoint on the matter.

"If Irvine's related to the child, why shouldn't he take him home?" Judith replied reasonably. "Maybe check with the school admin to see if he's listed as a contact."

"Good idea," she said and hung up.

The three of them hurried back into the school while Abbie explained to Jimi why she was worried. "I've never been introduced to River's uncle. Why weren't his parents here to watch over him?"

"They're on holiday. River said they've gone to Tooks and cakes. What's Tooks and cakes, Abbie?"

"Sound tasty," Nica offered, "if they get to eat cake."

Abbie stopped in her tracks. "I think that's maybe the Turks and Caicos Islands."

"Yes, that's it," Jimi said, nodding. "River's Uncle Shane entered them in a contest and they won the trip."

"Then it should be okay that he's gone with his uncle." She hesitated and, on instinct, said, "Just to be on the safe side, though, shall we check with the school admin as Judith suggested?"

"Sure," Nica agreed, half-heartedly, deflated at the lack of a proper hunt.

The clerk said that Shane Irvine was indeed in charge of River while the boy's parents were out of the country. That was that, then.

They returned to Rosie and sat in the car, pondering what to do next. Abbie wasn't in the mood to return to the school's activities. Without River, neither was Jimi.

"Want to go home for lunch?" Abbie asked.

"It's chores day," Nica reminded them in a cheerful voice. Abbie and Jimi rolled their eyes as Nica strapped herself into the front passenger seat, oblivious to their lackluster reaction. As of her last month's measurement, she'd grown tall enough, by law, to no longer need a car seat. But the girl had yet to outgrow her penchant for cleaning.

Abbie nodded acceptance of the plan and shifted her car into gear to leave the school. Yet, after being warned about River by the Hindu goddess and then learning the boy might be a supe, her Grimm instincts insisted that trouble was afoot.

She geared back into park. "I don't want to go home without checking up on your friend first," she murmured, thinking out loud.

"Yay!" Jimi said from his car seat, holding the two balloons. "River forgot to take his balloon, so I want to return his. Also, these balloons say I'm supposed to be with him."

Abbie turned around and frowned at the balloons. "Do they say why?"

Jimi shook his head. "They're creepy. They talk at the same time as if someone is talking to me through them. I don't like them. So fake."

A sudden loud *pop* inside the car made both kids squeal, while Abbie grinned with satisfaction. "Are they still talking to you, Jimi?"

Eyes wide, the boy shook his head. "Nope. Thanks, Abbie."

Alarmed by Jimi's summation of the balloons, Abbie had used her pocketknife to pop the two balloons.

She took both balloon remnants and strings, and getting out of the car, she chucked the lot into a nearby rubbish bin. Once back in Rosie, she attached her mobile to the dashboard and pulled up the GPS directions from the last time she had visited the Irvines. Must have been two months ago, now.

Abbie had the kids play the alphabet game while she drove, naming one item each child saw out the window, starting with A and then B, and so on. They'd reached K when she parked Rosie off the road by the Irvine home.

River's uncle had parked his gold Leaf in his driveway. Its driver's side door was ajar and the home's front door stood wide open.

Nica took Abbie's hand, clutching it.

"I'll be careful," she promised the little girl. "Both of you stay in the car."

After their reluctant nods, Abbie fetched her medical kit from the boot and locked the car. Cautiously, she approached the Irvine home, walking past Shane's parked golf.

Once beside the open front door, she called out, "Mr. Irvine, I'm Abigail Grimshaw. I'm the guardian of one of River's friends, Jimi Gill. May I speak to you, please?"

She waited.

No answer.

She peeked into the house. An empty entryway showed

scattered shoes and a half-open closet with coats hanging inside. Walls prevented her from seeing further.

"I'm coming in," she called out.

Silence.

Abbie alerted her Grimm cord to be ready to strike. It vibrated, twitching her right forefinger. She entered the house, clutching her medical kit in her dominant left hand, ready to use it, too, as a weapon if needed.

"River!" she called from the entryway. "Mr. Irvine? Anyone here?"

The lack of response was troubling.

In the living room, she came to a startled halt at finding Shane Irvine sitting in an armchair, looking up at her, his expression one of shock. The small, circular, bloody hole in the middle of his forehead and the blood splatters on the wall behind him said nothing in this world would shock him again.

An eerie sense of familiarity invaded Abbie. It seemed as if this was her life now. Finding a victim, even when she wasn't on Emergency Medical Technician duty.

At viewing this young Olympian, killed in the prime of his life, a profound sadness overcame Abbie. By rote, she gently checked for Shane Irvine's pulse, despite the hole in his forehead proclaiming him long gone. Not a beat.

The coppery stench of spilled blood made her cringe. She might as well have been underwater because she had to force herself to take a breath as her chest closed in and her throat tightened. The sense of death pervaded this room, vibrating like a siren's lament.

There was nothing else out of the ordinary here, except for the floor-to-ceiling fish tank against one wall. It held freshwater fish from carp to bass, and eels to mackerel. How had she missed seeing this on her last visit here? Unless it was a new acquisition?

Before leaving the room, she did a quick check for clues about the immediate crime scene. The room had little evidence that anyone other than a normal family, with an odd fetish for freshwater fish, lived here. No pet hair on cushions, curtains, or window sills. Family photos on the mantle. Kids' toys scattered about the room.

Where could River be? She hurried, checking the ground-floor rooms next, in case the boy was somewhere in this house, alive, hiding, waiting for help. Thankfully, the feeling of death didn't follow her. It seemed contained in that living room alone. River was nowhere in sight down here.

She headed upstairs, being careful to avoid leaving her fingerprints as she went from room to room in this two-story home. DI Turner, a rising star in Kent, would make it her business to follow up on this crime, simply because Abbie reported it. She didn't want to be accused of snooping, or worse. Turner wasn't her friend.

She found no one under beds or hiding inside the wardrobes upstairs. Abbie returned downstairs, certain the house was empty. Satisfied there was nothing else for her to find here, she wished Shane a sad goodbye and left as quietly as she had entered.

Abbie got into Rosie's driver's seat.

"Where is River?" Jimi asked in a fearful tone, ripping off his mask.

Not, *Is he okay?* Her boy would have heard from something in that house—perhaps from the house itself—that his friend wasn't inside. Also, whoever had been Jimi's informant didn't know where River had gone, or he wouldn't ask that question—he'd tell her where to find his friend.

She sent him a compassionate glance. "Do you know who might have taken him, Jimi?"

He shook his head.

Abbie nodded. "Wherever he is, we'll find him. This is now an SB case."

The circumstances fit their supernatural requirements. Jimi and River had pinkie squirted before the boy disappeared.

Abbie retrieved her mobile and called Judith. "Someone's killed Shane Irvine."

Her friend swore.

Abbie invited Nica to crawl onto her lap. She then extended her arm toward Jimi. He clutched it tight and began crying. "River Irvine is missing," she informed Judith. "His parents have to be notified and a Child Rescue Alert put out."

By the time Abbie hung up, Jimi had extracted himself from his car seat and crawled into the front to join his sister on Abbie's lap. She hugged both kids tight as they waited for the police and ambulance to arrive. She was shaking as much as her kids in reaction because it could so easily have been Jimi who was missing instead of poor River.

Chapter Two

While Abbie wrote out her statements at the Chipstead police station, Judith bought them all burgers and chips for lunch. At one point, DCI Callum Radford stopped by to speak to Abbie. It was an awkward meeting.

Last Autumn, Abbie explained to Callum about Figg, an immortal dog, and all the killing he had been responsible for over the centuries. She'd expected him to avoid the dangerous pup after that. Instead, he'd adopted Figg. Abbie couldn't understand that thinking and they'd had a royal row about it.

Her brother Bran suggested that for a norm, having a magical defender was too tempting a prospect to give up easily. Bran should know, since Judith had gifted him Comet, her magical broom, for his protection.

As hard as she tried, though, Abbie couldn't equate Comet to Figg. She liked Figg and Jimi loved him, but she didn't trust the dog. At his old master's command, the mutt had murdered people. Even if she had impressed on the dog the importance of not killing again, that didn't mean his old master couldn't compel him if the mood struck.

True, the immortal had slunk back into the underworld once COVID broke out, abandoning the dog here. That didn't mean he wouldn't eventually return for it.

Callum didn't see it that way. "I'm now responsible for Figg, and I won't abandon him like his previous master," had been his vehement response.

A commendable sentiment, but it put him in a tricky situation and potentially in the line of fire if trouble brewed.

They'd ended up at an impasse that put any chance of a relationship between them on ice, yet again. Abbie had been heartsore for weeks after that stark conversation, listening for her phone, hoping it was Callum calling.

He never called.

She shook off that lingering regret, but her heart still ached at seeing him again. Once she and her kids returned home, she put off their Saturday chores and instead allowed the kids to take a well-needed nap.

Still a little rattled at how close Jimi had come to going off with River and his uncle, Abbie couldn't tear herself from their side yet. Instead, she called Klaus, her Grimm Tales, to her in the kids' room and asked the book about River's whereabouts.

Klaus flipped open his pages until he came to a colorful drawing of a market called Spell Gate. This bazaar was also an access point to otherworldly beings, who bought and sold all manner of unusual items there. Various compounds existed all around the market to house different species while they visited. This practice had been ongoing for time immemorial. The book didn't show her River, merely different stalls and locations around the market.

Where the market appeared on Earth routinely changed. It came to cities or towns or villages across the world at irregular intervals to ensure normal humans never stumbled across it.

As fascinating as all this information was, why would Klaus choose that market to show her when she'd asked about River? Unless someone had taken the boy there. Unfortunately, there was no information about how to get to this market.

She posted a quick note on her podcast to ask if anyone had heard of the Spell Gate market. If so, leave a comment.

Her followers rarely corresponded with her, and if they did, the ones who wrote in turned out to be ordinary humans with more curiosity than sense. Still, it was worth a shot.

Her gaze kept swerving to the sleeping children. She wished Robert were here to talk to. She'd not seen him since last night. This was his time to grieve his daughter, and she wasn't about to disturb that by calling to him.

She nodded off with the open book on her lap.

Abbie awoke to find Jimi still asleep, but Nica's bed was empty and neatly made up. It was twilight and someone had tucked a blanket around Abbie.

A quick furtive check located Nica wiping down the shelves and windowsills in the living room downstairs. Abbie's heart did a flip of joy at seeing her girl safe and busy. She suspected Nica needed to do something after their stressful day. So, Abbie sat on the stairs and watched her through the living room door left slightly ajar. Soon, Jimi joined her, leaning against Abbie's side, yawning.

She gave him a long hug until he squirmed out of her hold. Then she set him to empty all the bins in the house into a big black bag left open on the kitchen floor and went to get the laundry running and then cleaned the loo. Nica wasn't the only one who felt the need to be busy on this troublesome day.

Mentally, she added dusting St. Michael's church to her to-do list for tomorrow, after she dropped the kids at the Hindu temple for service. She would have to skip church service with her mum this Sunday, though, as Abbie needed time to prepare for her First Aid class on Monday. It would be the first lesson held at St. Michael's church. She'd readied lecture notes, but needed to adjust the classroom set-up.

After Callum fixed up the abandoned church last year, all of England had gone under lockdown as COVID spread again. That prevented Abbie from utilizing the space, even if she could have afforded to buy supplies to run the classes.

This year, the government sent out financial help because of the lockdowns. Abbie also continued to work part-time as an EMT. In addition, her child support payments finally flowed in. All of that cash inflow meant she could afford to buy supplies to conduct first-aid classes. She was super excited to begin and had already scored ten registrants.

Once she and the kids completed their Saturday chores, she made a quick light evening meal before they headed upstairs to the kids' room.

Robert appeared there, looking haggard and worn. Nica ran over to give him a hug and Jimi joined in. Robert's resultant radiant smile said more than anything that this ghost was ready to return to the living.

The first words out of Jimi's mouth were that his friend was missing.

After Robert chided Abbie for not contacting him earlier, she brought him up-to-date on what had happened this morning. That reminded her again of how close she'd come to losing Jimi. Until they solved who had taken Jimi's friend, the kids needed to take more precautions.

"Nica, Jimi," Abbie said, "bring out your bracelets and sword. Until we find River, wear those items."

As soon as they'd grabbed them, Arthur, her pen-ring, magically linked to the two toys, and from there extended the ring's protection over the children. After they'd finished that procedure, Abbie tucked the kids in and read a story from

Klaus until the two fell asleep.

• • • •

ABBIE CALLED AN SB meeting for Sunday afternoon to discuss this newest case. After she drove the kids home from temple, they sprawled on the sofa in the living room, discussing what to have for lunch when the doorbell rang.

Robert looked out the living room window. "Detective Constable Chan is here."

Ever since Judith received news that she'd passed her exams, he'd begun calling her by her new title. Judith had worked hard to become a detective, and she lit up every time he addressed her as such.

Jimi didn't yell, "Yay," and run for the door to greet her, however, which said much about the lad's broken heart.

Once Abbie let Judith in, her friend said she was famished. Abbie mentioned a chicken dish they'd decided on for lunch, and they all reconvened in the kitchen.

Cooking had become her kids' favorite activity after Granny Chan's stay here last year during the lockdown, while Abbie roomed with Judith. The elderly witch had ensured both kids mastered the basics of cooking and knew how to make some excellent dishes.

Judith made lunch with the kids' help. While Robert and Abbie set the table, while Judith updated them on how the search for River progressed.

Kneeling on a chair by the counter as he expertly snapped beans, Jimi listened intently.

Nica tended to a fried rice dish on the cooktop.

A vegetable dish was also stewing in the oven for Yousef,

their only vegan member.

He arrived at her door next and handed Abbie a beautiful fragrant flower bouquet in an array of golds and yellows.

"How nice," she said, truly pleased. They all needed a little cheering up. "We're in the kitchen. Talin isn't here yet."

"He didn't come with Judith?" he asked, following her.

"Said he'd received an S999 hit this morning, which he wanted to verify wasn't a crank call."

That's all they'd been in the past on her supe emergency line linked to her podcast, so this time was unlikely to be different. Like witches, other supes in England distrusted Abbie to be on their side. Grimms had a long history, not only in England but worldwide, of vanquishing supes in the name of protecting the greater good. Such old fears were hard to shake.

It pleased her, though, that the number of her podcast followers had grown over the last two years. They now numbered in the thousands.

Abbie and her friends were all well into their meal, discussing Klaus's revelation about the Spell Gate market, when the wards surrounding her home sent up an alert.

Then the doorbell rang.

"I'll check," she said, waving everyone else down. It had to be Talin, but the ward's reaction said he hadn't come alone. Despite telling herself there was little hope the S999 call was legitimate, a small part of her hoped it had panned out.

With them already on the River case, though, would they have time for another SB case?

"Shields," she told Arthur, and it sprang up before she'd opened the front door.

It was indeed Talin on the other side. Past his shoulder, she spotted a young woman by her picket fence and recognized her. River's mother, Mrs. Vivian Irvine. She had set off the house's ward, which prevented unknown supes from entering, but not ordinary humans. Interesting.

"Isn't she supposed to be in Turks and Caicos with her husband?" she whispered to Talin.

"As soon as we notified River's parents yesterday that their son was missing and Shane Irvine was dead," Talin said, "they both rushed home. Mrs. Irvine's also the one who hit our S999. Will you allow her in?"

Abbie strode out to the edge of the wards and laid her hand on the invisible barrier, adjusting it to allow her unexpected guest to enter. She nodded to show it was safe to approach and then led the lady toward the house.

This was the first supe ever to ask for the Standard Bearers' help. She certainly qualified under their "dire trouble" criteria. If they could help Mrs. Irvine, it might open the door to other supes trusting them. If they failed, that door might slam shut.

Mrs. Vivian Irvine was exactly as Abbie recalled her from a few months ago when Abbie contrived an introduction with the family. A wavy-haired brunette with a sultry figure that made men sit up with eagerness and women's shoulders straighten with reserve. She had an exquisite sharp-boned face with flinty, teal eyes.

Her unsmiling face and demeanor came across as lofty. Mother and son were similar in that respect, except this woman lacked her son's disarming freckles and Jimi's endorsement. Her son had described River as someone who was "chill and could make outstanding noises," so worthy of his trust.

"I need your help, Miss Grimshaw," her guest said, her

sultry voice flowing like a hot spring.

"Call me Abbie."

"I'm Vivian."

"Hello," Jimi said from beside Talin.

Abbie glanced down in surprise. He must have followed her out of the kitchen, and she hadn't even noticed. Entering the house, she placed a protective hand on his shoulder.

Vivian's face and stance softened. "Hello, Jimi."

In the kitchen, Talin made introductions while Abbie brought in a spare chair for their guest. The lady declined a plate of food.

Judith assured her that the police were doing everything they could to find her son.

Sitting quietly observing Vivian, Abbie did something she should when she visited her two months ago, but hadn't. She shifted her sight to really "see" the lady. Her aura immediately came alive, a bright blue with an azure highlight that flowed around her like a stream. Stunning. Definitely a supe. This was why she had triggered the wards.

"Forgive me for asking," Yousef said, "but how is this a supernatural case for the Standard Bearers?"

Good question!

Jimi, who was sitting beside Abbie, looked ready to speak up, his lips opening. Blinking to clear her vision, Abbie placed a warning hand on his arm. A shake of her head and he closed his mouth and sat back.

The lady's gaze fell to her hands, which were fidgeting on her lap. When she looked up, her cautious gaze roved to meet each of their stares, including Robert's, at whom she stared the longest, before returning to Yousef.

Releasing a deep breath, she finally said, "River can manipulate water."

"That's how he could pinkie squirt," Abbie said, nodding in understanding. That fish tank in their bedroom also made sense. As did her undulating aura. This family had a strong water connection.

River could call water to him, so Vivian, too, must possess water powers. Was she a witch? Wizard? Sorceress? Or was she not human at all? Could she be a fae? Or something else entirely? Hard to tell from a simple aura reading.

One of the five immortal Companions was a water being. He'd helped Abbie recover a sunken vessel. Could Vivian be from his realm? A fascinating possibility.

"My son can do a few things with water," Mrs. Irvine said, "small things. Nothing that should startle a norm. I taught him to be careful among strangers. The only one he ever confided in about his powers is Jimi."

Vivian turned to the boy. "Do you know if River told you about anyone interested in his ability?"

"Just his Uncle Shane," Jimi said.

Vivian's eyes widened as if that was news.

"Did your brother-in-law not know about River's water ability?" Judith asked, having also noticed their guest's reaction to Jimi's news about Shane Irvine.

Vivian shook her head. "It's not something we talk about with anyone, not even close family."

"Your husband knows?" Abbie pressed.

"Yes."

The lady was tight-lipped. "Is Mr. Irvine a supe as well?"

"No."

Like pulling teeth. But if her husband wasn't a supe, then Shane would have also been a norm. "Your husband wasn't close enough to his brother to confide in him?"

"They were close," Vivian said, frowning. "My husband was the one who encouraged Shane to apply to join the Olympics. Seamus is an excellent dive coach and trained his brother for the upcoming competition. When they cut Shane from the team earlier this summer, it devastated them both. That's why my husband asked Shane to stay with us awhile, to make sure his brother wouldn't slide into depression."

"Why did your husband not accompany you tonight?" Robert asked, standing behind Abbie.

"He's manning our landline," Vivian said, "in case someone calls there about River or drops by. He's taken a few days off to be around while I work with you to locate my son."

The gaze she sent to Abbie was a firm, no-nonsense one that said Abbie couldn't talk Vivian into leaving the case in their hands.

"Vivian," Judith said, "in your statement this morning, you said that no one has contacted you or your husband with a ransom note for your son. Has that changed?"

"Whoever took my boy," Vivian said in a firm voice, "doesn't want to extort us. River is different. A child with supernatural ability. That's why they took him."

"What makes you so certain?" Judith asked.

Vivian pointed toward her heart. "I know it here. My boy is frightened, and he's not the only one."

"What do you mean?" Judith leaned forward with concern. "Who else is involved in this?"

"I see vague flashes. River seems to be in a cage and there

may be other children in adjacent pens."

Abbie glanced at the other Standard Bearers with alarm. More than one child was missing? The description brought to mind her other clue to this case. The magical market Klaus showed her.

An abominable thought followed on the heels of that. What if that market bought and sold more than magical objects and herbs? What if they trafficked in magical children, too?

"Have you ever heard of a market called Spell Gate?" Abbie asked Vivian.

For the first time, a faint blush stained Vivian's pale cheeks, and her gaze flicked away.

"I texted Gran about that market," Judith said. "She confirmed that it's a supernatural market. It's where supes barter for magical hard-to-find items."

"It's a multi-dimensional magical market," Vivian put in. "Creatures from different realms enter at different times. There are strict rules and barriers to realm travel, so this market is the only way for different realm inhabitants to co-mingle."

"I suspect someone in there," Abbie said, "perhaps a vendor, knows something about where River is being held."

Why else would Klaus have shown her the market?

Just then, Talin's phone pinged, as did Judith's. They both checked their mobiles.

"Is it news about my son?" Vivian asked, anxious.

"There's a problem with the Child Rescue Alert system," Talin said. "The CRA has become overloaded with crank calls. Uncle Cal wants me to return to the office and help work on the problem. He thinks someone's infiltrated the alerts to distract us."

"He wants all hands on deck," Judith said, "in case one or more of those calls turn out to be genuine leads." She glanced at Vivian. "I'll contact you if any pan out."

"Thank you," their guest said with sincere gratitude.

Once the two left the kitchen, Abbie steered the conversation back to the previous topic. "Vivian, how do you access this market?"

"When it's on Earth, supes can enter from various doorways from around the world. The market gatekeeper notifies trusted travelers of when and where to enter." Her wary glance settled on Abbie, before she added, "There's a doorway in Kent."

"When is this market scheduled to arrive next?"

"It arrived here on Friday," Vivian said. "When it comes, it's usually on a weekend, with a twenty-four-hour buffer on either side."

"That explains why River was snatched on Saturday," Abbie said.

Vivian leaned forward. "The market will remain here until Monday night. But if we miss this window to enter, we'll have to wait a month before it returns."

Giving her guest a lead to follow had been the key to opening a floodgate of information.

"I'd like to visit this magical market and nose around," Abbie said.

"Impossible," Vivian said, sitting back and crossing her arms. "Grimms are forbidden entry into Spell Gate."

Ah, that must be why she'd hesitated to share information about how to enter it.

Jimi tugged at Abbie's shirt sleeve.

"What is it, Jimi?" she asked.

"I could get us into the market," he said. "If I talk to the market, it may not tell on Abbie," Jimi said in a stubborn voice. "It would listen to me. I know it would."

That was a shocking concept and a tempting one.

"No!" Nica cried in fright, grabbing his hand. "You mustn't go. They might steal you, too."

"Agreed." Abbie put her arm around him to soften the blow of that rejection. He wanted to help his friend, a cause with which she deeply sympathized. "The answer is no, love."

"Your sister and Miss Grimshaw are correct in this," Robert said to Jimi. He sounded pleased by Abbie and Nica's vehement protest about the boy entering the Spell Gate market. "Best if you stay far from that market."

"People on the hunt for magical children might frequent there, Jimi," she explained to the deeply disappointed boy. "Even with Arthur's protection, I don't want you anywhere near that place. You've already been warned that they're on the lookout for you."

"What do you mean?" Vivian asked.

Abbie glanced at her and said, "The boys won two balloons at school yesterday. The balloons spoke to Jimi, saying he was to follow River. If he had, they could have taken him, too." She paused. "Those balloons met an untimely end."

Vivian sat back, her shoulders stiffening, as if Abbie's casual comment had brought out all her fears about working with a Grimm.

Chapter Three

"No one can get a Grimm into the Spell Gate market," Vivian said, reiterating her earlier point.

Jimi offering to get her in had given Abbie an idea. "I wonder if Hafgufa could persuade the market to make an exception this time?" she mused aloud.

"How are you connected to the lost goddess?" Vivian asked, sitting up, her eyes opening wide with surprise.

Abbie knew her cord was a goddess, but how did this woman? She'd asked Klaus about Hafgufa, but all the book said was that it had no more information than what Hafgufa had revealed to Abbie.

After considering how much to reveal to Vivian, Abbie decided that trust engendered trust.

"Hafgufa is my Grimm cord," she said. "What do you know about this goddess?" The cord twitched within her right arm as if she were paying attention. For a talkative being that loved to broadcast to all nearby, Hafgufa had been unusually reticent about revealing her past.

"She's a fallen goddess," Vivian said. "We pass down her tale in my family because she's the patron goddess of water beings." She then clamped her lips tight.

Said too much? Closest Vivian had come to revealing that she was as magical as her son.

"My cord could convince the market to open its doors," Abbie said. "She is persuasive."

Vivian's stiff shoulder loosened. "Makes sense, since she's a water goddess." As Abbie's eyebrow raised in inquiry, she added, "Water is a mode of communication." After another hesitation, her voice cracking and eyes tearing, she added, "That's why I can see my boy. There's a puddle near where he's being held. I see him reflected there."

"What else do you know about the Goddess Hafgufa?" Robert asked. He was being kind in changing the subject as Vivian looked ready to break down talking about her son.

The lady cleared her throat before speaking. "It's said that she killed a god, and the other gods punished her."

Abbie's cord flared within her arm, before subsiding, as if annoyed by that speculation.

Whatever Hafgufa's take on what had happened in her past, this story lined up with Klaus's record that her Grimm cord could kill gods.

"What was the punishment?" Abbie asked, lowering her right arm before it flared so brightly everyone noticed.

"No one knows, but shortly after the incident, all records of her activities ceased."

"Who did she kill?" Robert asked.

"It's said she doused the god of fire," Vivian said with a quirk of her lips. No sympathy there for the demise of this fire god. Abbie's cord didn't move within her arm, leaving her wondering if the story could be true.

"Both fire and water sprites have been growing uncontrollable ever since," Vivian said. "Whenever a human ignites a fire sprite, often inadvertently, there are few around who can easily temper it. That's why you hear about so many uncontrollable fires around the world. As for the water sprites, they've been flooding streets and towns for centuries trying to find their goddess."

"You won't tell them where she is?" Abbie asked in worry.

Vivian shook her head. "Not my place. The goddess will speak to her subjects when she's ready."

That answer brought up a thousand new questions, but Yousef interrupted by asking, "Shall we give your cord a try, Abbie? See if Hafgufa can help us break into the market?"

"It won't work," Vivian said, shutting down that plan before it could gather steam. "The moment it touches the door, the market will vanish. There'll be nothing there to persuade."

"I could go in feline form," Yousef said. "That should prove innocuous enough to allow me entrance."

"You're the cat shifter?" Vivian said. "I've been following your podcast for months." Her glance swerved to Abbie, and she flashed a tiny smile, the first to touch her lips tonight. "Most everyone in the supe community does."

Welcome news to Abbie. Yet, sending Yousef by himself didn't appeal. "I don't like you going without backup."

"He won't be alone," Vivian said. "I'll be with him."

Abbie didn't know enough about Vivian's abilities to gauge if that was enough support for Yousef. Was she even trustworthy? In a magical fight, everyone needed a reliable partner. With Talin and Judith unavailable, and Abbie unable to enter the market, that left no other SB member free, unless Robert could go with them. Except, aside from accompanying Abbie to places, the ghost had only manifested at St. Michael's.

"We'll have to wait until the morning," Vivian continued. "The market's unsafe to approach at night. That's when those who practice dark arts, powerful supes, and aliens frequent the market. For now, my boy is safe. They've already locked up the place where he's being held."

"The children and I should be able to follow both of your movements using Klaus," Abbie said. "The book showed me your activities once before, Yousef. I don't know how much help I can be, but if there's anything I can do, maybe through Klaus, I will. Are you sure about this?"

He nodded. "Children are in danger. I swore I wouldn't ever allow what happened to me to happen to any other child, not if I could help it."

"Thank you, Yousef." Jimi ran around the table to hug him. Nica joined him.

Yousef held both close. "We'll find River and bring him home safe. And any other child there. Believe it."

"Come to my home Monday at sunrise," Vivian said, "and I'll drive us to the market portal."

Yousef agreed, and the children returned to their seats.

Vivian rose. "I'll notify my husband and clients that I'll be away tomorrow."

Abbie made a mental note to postpone her First-Aid class. That would have to wait until this case was resolved. She rose as well, to escort her guest out.

Instead of heading to the door, Vivian came around the table, approaching Jimi.

Robert and Abbie moved aside, and the boy looked up. Abbie held her breath, wondering what she was up to.

Vivian hesitated a moment. Then she moved her hand toward Jimi, hovering over his plastic King Arthur's sword. Did she sense its invisible presence? Her glance swung toward Abbie. "May I?"

"May you what?" Abbie asked.

"If they are after Jimi, too, this will give him a bit of added protection. I wish I'd done more for my boy before we left on our holiday."

"That sword already protects Jimi," Abbie said, but couldn't help seriously considering her offer. She glanced at Nica and Jimi to get their take. Both children nodded their heads emphatically in agreement. Nica wanted her brother protected and Jimi must feel insecure after losing his friend.

A bit of extra protection couldn't hurt. She glanced back at Vivian and her Grimm senses gave assurance that Vivian meant no ill will. Satisfied with that—she trusted her Grimm sense to lead her true—she nodded and sent Arthur a message to allow Vivian access to the sword.

Her guest focused on the now visible sword. For a moment, it flashed, its hilt appearing to fit snugly within Vivian's grip and the plastic blade glistening as if soaked. Then she released it and the sword vanished. "That should do it."

"Thank you," Jimi said, smiling.

Vivian bent and whispered in his ear, and then she hurried out of Abbie's cottage.

Abbie walked her guest to the other side of the warded white picket gate. Shortly after, the SB meeting disbanded. She and the kids took a trip to her parents' pub and helped them set up for the evening session. Her mother told Jimi she was certain they would get River home soon. Abbie doubted he believed her. Once back home, they watched telly while digesting the day's troubling events.

Abbie had been waiting all afternoon for Jimi to mention what Vivian had whispered to him, but he didn't say a word about it. Finally, as they readied for bed and brushed their teeth in the downstairs loo, she casually asked him about it.

"I'm to draw the sword only if I need it desperately." His words slurped out of a mouth full of foamy toothpaste.

"I wonder why she didn't feel safe to say that aloud?" Abbie mused. "Does the sword feel any different?"

Jimi shook his head and spit out paste. "Nope. But it says it now has a name. Caleb."

"Cool," Nica said from beside him.

They reconvened in the children's bedroom.

Robert stood by the window, looking out back, the only one still formally dressed from frock coat to breeches and Hessians. The kids were in their PJs, tucked under bedsheets, while Abbie, with Klaus open to a bedtime story, sat on a chair in her night clothes of a large T-shirt, shorts, and a robe.

The tale she'd picked for tonight was about a mage's visit to the Spell Gate market. He was hunting for a rare ingredient to cure a friend of a magical wound. He'd heard that a dawn-time fae vendor at the market might carry it.

• • • •

AT SIX THE NEXT MORNING, Abbie propped up Klaus on the kitchen table so they could all watch Vivian and Yousef as they navigated to the Spell Gate market.

Vivian hadn't specified exactly where, simply saying it was in a public location. That description brought to mind the *Harry Potter* movies of stepping between platforms at a train station. Would they go down a lane into a mysterious wall? Abbie could hardly wait to see this play out in Klaus.

Today was the first day of the kids' summer holidays. In celebration, she made pancakes, her mother's recipe. They were thicker than crepes, but thinner than store-bought branded versions. Perfect for a light breakfast.

As they dug into their meal, Klaus showed Yousef parking Shahay, his nitro yellow Toyota Supra, on the Irvine's drive. His fae-car was the jealous type and hated when he drove in any other vehicle. Not surprising to hear Shahay honk in outrage as he got into Vivian's car and it backed up with Yousef lounging beside Vivian in his cat form.

Robert stood behind the kids, watching the car depart.

"Abbie," Nica said, "Jimi and I want to talk to you about something."

Jimi nodded, his gaze on Abbie rather than the book.

Nica was halfway through her meal, while Jimi's plate was empty. He was a fast eater.

"They've arrived at a shopping center," Robert said, pointing to Klaus. "Rather an odd spot for the entrance of a secret market."

Everyone glanced over to where Vivian had parked her vehicle at the Sevenoaks shopping center.

"Maybe they went there to pick up snacks for the trip," Jimi mused, his gaze returning to his empty plate.

Abbie pushed her remaining pancakes onto his plate and he nodded his thanks, reaching for the fruit jam.

"Neither of them has exited the carriage," Robert added. "Could there be a specific time to enter the location?"

A bad feeling rose in Abbie. Her Grimm instincts said something was about to happen, but she didn't know what.

Gigantic claws appeared above the vehicle and clamped onto the roof. Then the car and claw vanished. Just like that, they lost track of both Yousef and Vivian.

"Uh, oh!" Jimi said, his pancakes forgotten.

An understatement! "Klaus," Abbie said, her anxiety rising, "show us where they've ended up inside the market."

The picture in the book remained on the shopping center's empty parking spot and Abbie's stomach plummeted. Why couldn't Klaus show her the market today, when he'd done it yesterday? Unless that had been a generic view. Maybe he couldn't show her anything specific or current.

Robert met her worried glance.

The children looked at each other and then over at her. "Abbie, we've been talking."

"About what?" she asked, turning her distracted gaze toward the children.

Nica took Jimi's hand. "You always tell us we shouldn't run from trouble. That we should face it."

Pacing around the table, Robert paused, his face blanching.

Abbie sympathized with his reaction. She didn't like where this conversation seemed to be headed.

"We want to go to the Spell Gate market, too," Nica finished in a rush. "Especially if River, Mrs. Irvine, and Yousef are now in trouble in there."

"We don't know if Yousef and Vivian are in trouble yet," Abbie said, but once they voiced their desire, her anxiety decreased. In its place rose an overwhelming sense of pride for her brave kids. They'd come such a long way since the night she found them cowering in terror beside their mother's body. Also, their desire perfectly matched hers. She, too, wanted to go to the market to find Yousef, Vivian, and River.

"I have an idea," Abbie said, meeting Robert's concerned gaze. "Let's check with Levi, my Grimm compass, again. I tried using him to locate River yesterday and he couldn't, but he's proven he's good at finding Yousef. He could do it again, and if he can find Yousef, that might help us track down River."

She jumped up and ran up out of the kitchen. The children were right at her heels. They arrived in her bedroom to find Robert already present. He'd unearthed her rucksack from under her bed and set it on top of her sheets.

Abbie sat beside it, and the kids joined her. She opened the bag, inhaling odd scents from burnt smoke, old paper, and rusty pipes. Occasionally, she'd even scented a whiff of cinnamon and myrrh rising from in here, but not today.

As usual, an effervescing sense of friendship, adventure, and excitement accompanied the scents. A reminder that her ancestors had been gifted these items during their supernatural adventures.

As Jimi and Nica looked on, Abbie reached in and caused a clatter and startled mutterings from the items as she sorted through them until she found the compass.

"Levi." Abbie pictured Yousef, from his handsome Arabian features to his unusually striking blue eyes beneath his glasses. "Where is Yousef?"

Levi's needles swung.

Last year, when they sought Yousef after he went missing, Talin primed this compass to triangulate using St. Michael's steeple as a touchpoint.

It used that now. Except, this time, the needles kept swinging, but didn't settle in any direction.

"Levi can't find him," Jimi said, mirroring Abbie's fears. "He says he's sorry."

She gave a defeated sigh, for she'd heard those words, too, because she'd been holding the item and her Grimm cord had communicated with Levi.

"This market could be in a different dimension," Robert said.

"Klaus partly exists in another realm, too," Abbie said, deeply disappointed. "So, if he can't track Yousef's movements, it's not surprising that Levi failed."

They sat in silence, running through their options.

"Wait," Abbie said. "Why don't we try this a different way? If we can't find Yousef or River, maybe we can help the police locate whoever kidnapped River by finding where they had taken him before taking him into the market."

She pictured the young freckled-faced boy who'd scowled at her on Saturday because she'd put a kibosh on him and Jimi cheating in the egg-and-spoon game. "Levi, after someone snatched River from his home yesterday, where did they take him?"

The needles swung, but this time, one stopped right away, and then the second and third.

They stared at the compass in shock.

Even though Abbie had asked for this information, she couldn't believe her gamble had worked. Levi could identify where they'd taken River. Though the likelihood of the perpetrators still being there was slim, the kids needed to be doing something to solve this mystery. It wasn't far from here.

She met Jimi's excited gaze, and then Nica's, and said, "Okay. Let's check out this place. In case there are any other children there that need help."

"Yes!" both children shouted.

The three of them ran for the door.

"Wait," Robert said, soberly.

Abbie turned back, impatient to be on the hunt. "What's wrong?"

Her kids, too, returned to the room.

"What do we do if we locate a child in trouble?" Robert asked.

"We call 999 and wait outside for the police to come," she replied, quoting Judith's order if Abbie was ever in trouble.

"What if that's impossible because the child is in immediate danger?" Robert persisted. He pointed to Abbie's rucksack on the bed. "In case something delays the police, an artifact in here might help us safeguard the child until they come."

Abbie returned to the bed, recalling the long lonely wait for help to arrive at St. Michael's on the night the kids' mother died. Today, nuisance calls had been overwhelming the police, so who knew when they would come?

Back then, she hadn't been aware of these magnificent artifacts gifted to her family, or even the fact that she was a Grimm. She had used quite a few since. The cord and pen-ring had merged with her. On every Grimm adventure since, she'd tried out a new item.

Usually at Robert's instigation. Wise man.

This was an excellent opportunity to test out another item. The more artifacts she familiarized herself with, the better use she could put them to when the time came to face her "enemy" from the Grimm prophecy.

She could take the entire bag, but she preferred to keep these valuable items within this warded house, rather than leave them unguarded in her car.

"Which one should I take?" she pondered aloud.

"A wish bomb?" Jimi asked, hurrying back to her side.

His favorite item. The worst, in Abbie's view, since it destroyed indiscriminately. One had been used to attack Judith. She shuddered and pushed aside that terrifying memory. She'd almost lost her brother, Bran, too, then. The point was, Abbie had already seen that artifact at work.

She sat on the bed and peered into her rucksack. "I want something I haven't tried before."

"Jimi, you ask them," Nica suggested, coming over to get things moving.

"Good idea," Abbie said.

"They're all talking," Jimi reported.

Every one of these could consider itself special and of use to her, and rightly so. She waved her hand over the chatter-box items. "Shhh."

Jimi nodded, affirming all had gone quiet.

"Now," she said, "which one of you can help us rescue a child today?" She turned to Jimi. "Anyone speak up?"

Jimi listened and then shook his head in the negative. The silence lengthened. Then Jimi leaned over and pointed. "Maybe that one." He pulled out a hand-sized mirror and handed it to Abbie. "She says her name is Ruth, and she wants to be of service."

Abbie eagerly accepted the artifact. Ruth had a glass frame and a handle in the shape of a mermaid. Appropriate for this water-sensitive case. "Hello, Ruth."

"Hello!" Hafgufa transmitted Ruth's answer. She had a sing-song voice, soft and shy.

"What do you do, Ruth?" Abbie asked the mirror.

"I can make you look like anyone you want or no one."

"Wow!" Nica said, impressed.

Her response confirmed that Hafgufa had spoken to all. Abbie had given up lecturing the cord about that. Hafgufa was a water goddess, and she spoke to whomever she pleased.

"I'd love to do that at school!" Nica added.

"Do what?" Abbie asked.

"Be no one," Nica replied, "so I can see what people think and say when they don't think I'm there."

Odd wish. She made a mental note to speak to Nica about where that urge came from later. Right now, finding out who'd taken their missing friends was their priority.

"It would be great if we weren't noticed during our spy mission," she said and winked at Robert. "Almost as good as being a ghost."

He gave her an acknowledging head tilt, and she tucked the mirror into her leather jacket pocket. She expected it to stick out, but it slid right out of sight. When she patted the pocket, she couldn't feel its presence, but sensed it was still there. Well and good.

Abbie tucked her rucksack under the bed. Rising, she said, "Let's go."

"Yay!" the kids shouted, and beat her out the door.

Robert vanished before Abbie left the room and she guessed she'd find him in Rosie's front passenger seat before Nica could claim it. It was a game they'd been playing since the young girl outgrew her car seat.

Chuckling, Abbie sprinted downstairs after her kids and out of the house.

Chapter Four

Out in front of St. Michael's church, Abbie backed away from where she'd parked Rosie. From habit, her glance shot up to the three-paneled windows on the church's front wall. Years ago, there used to be three beautiful stained-glass windows in those panels. The first depicted the birth of Christ. The middle one showed his death. And the last, his resurrection.

When Abbie was about her kids' ages, she used to pay illicit visits to this abandoned church. There, she had always admired an angel that hovered above baby Jesus in that first panel. Sometimes, she even spoke to her, telling her about an argument she'd had with a schoolmate or an unfair reprimand from a teacher. The angel never responded, but Abbie always felt listened to.

One day, the skinflint Earl of Ashford sold those panels off and boarded up the windows. Last year, when Callum renovated St. Michael's for Abbie, he'd replaced the boards with plain glass panels. For the first time in years, natural light now flowed into the church's recesses.

Abbie was grateful for his work, but when she looked at the see-through glass, she sometimes still saw the angel up there. As she did now. She blinked, and the panel turned back to plain glass. She gave a shiver at that poignant memory and drove out of St. Michael's car park.

The drive took them out of Chipstead and towards Sevenoaks. That surprised Abbie. She thought Levi would guide them toward the countryside, perhaps a secluded, wooded area devoid of crowds. A place to avoid awkward questions about why unsupervised children were gathering.

Instead, the compass led them toward an urban setting, with heavy vehicle and pedestrian traffic. They finally stopped before a large recital hall.

Abbie, Robert, and the kids sat quietly gazing at the building in stunned surprise. She'd brought her kids here last Christmas to enjoy a choir. It was also a favorite spot for local schools to hold children's recitals. Why would River's kidnappers bring him here?

"Okay," Abbie said. "You three stay in Rosie and keep a lookout while I check out this place." She glanced at Robert. "Let me know if anyone arrives while I'm inside."

He nodded.

"I want to come," Jimi said. "I can ask items in that hall if they've seen River."

"If Jimi goes, I want to come, too," Nica replied.

"I do not advise that," Robert said in a firm tone.

Abbie glanced back at Jimi, whose eyes were fiercely determined. He'd already unhooked his seat belt. He intended to save his friend at all costs.

"Jimi," she said and waited until his gaze met hers and held steady. "You spoke to River's house earlier," she reminded him. "Think you can do the same to that hall? Ask if River has been around here recently."

Jimi's eyes widened as if that simple solution had not occurred. His gaze swerved to the hall, and he concentrated, gaze unwavering. After a moment, he shouted, "Tell me!"

Nica reached out and took Jimi's hand in concern, her worried gaze catching Abbie's startled one as she took in a wave of energy shooting out from Jimi.

Across the road, the recital hall trembled and dust clouds rose around the surrounding grounds as if Jimi had physically shaken the hall. People on the street cried out in alarm and ducked and glanced up as if expecting structures to fall on them. Shouts of "earthquake" rang out.

Jimi flashed Abbie a triumphant grin. "He's not there now, but River was here earlier. The hall didn't want to tell me, but I said it must."

Every word Jimi spoke hit Abbie like successive shock waves from that non-existent earthquake.

The hall had resisted answering Jimi's question?

Jimi had overridden that resistance?

"Stay put," she said to Jimi and locked the car doors to be certain to keep the excited boy in place. It wouldn't hold him once he figured out he could talk the car into unlocking its doors. It should slow him down for Robert to intervene. She tapped her mobile on the dashboard to call Judith.

"What's up?" her law enforcement friend asked.

As Abbie gave Judith the address to the hall, an SUV pulled up to the building's long drive and parked. The driver exited and, glancing around, headed toward the rear. On spotting Abbie staring at him from across the street, he jerked to a halt, his eyes bugging. Then he hot-footed it back into his SUV, reversed, and sped off.

Before she lost sight of him down the road, with wheels screeching, Abbie pulled into the busy street. "Buckle up and hang on," she called, and swerved around a vehicle. That driver honked at her close call.

"There are children inside that carriage," Robert said in

alarm. He vanished and appeared inside the car ahead. Abbie sped up to keep from losing the fast-moving SUV. She grabbed her mobile from her dashboard and tossed it over her shoulder. "Nica, let Judith know what's happening."

Around the next bend, she read out the vehicle number plate for Nica to pass on.

The SUV swerved around the streets of Sevenoaks and then it headed into a shopping center. The same one where Vivian and Yousef had vanished. By the time they tracked the SUV down in the car park, they found it parked in the same spot where Vivian's car had vanished. As they pulled up beside it, gigantic talons grabbed the SUV and they all disappeared.

"Robert," she called, worried he might have become trapped in the Spell Gate market with that SUV.

"I am here," he said, appearing beside her in the front passenger seat, but none too happy about it.

Abbie's sigh of relief quickly changed to horror as realization set in on what this meant. They'd lost not only the SUV but those children in it. "Were the children his?"

"A boy and a girl," he said, sounding as horrified as she felt. "They were unconscious. I could not wake them, Miss Grimshaw. I returned to report my finding when the claw took the vehicle." He let loose a shuddering breath. "I should have stayed with them."

"We will find them," Abbie said, to reassure herself and those with her. A glance in the mirror showed Jimi and Nica in tears and holding hands. This was a stark reminder of the others who were now lost in the Spell Gate market.

On impulse, Abbie backed up her car and then drove in to park Rosie in the exact spot where the Spell Gate market claw had snatched the other two vehicles.

Neither children nor Robert objected to this bold move.

Nica could call on a god when in trouble and Jimi could talk to any object nearby to come to his aid when needed. And at seven and ten years of age, her kids were both growing up fast, and were no longer willing to be coddled.

Meanwhile, she had Arthur on her left ring finger to defend all three. Also, Hafgufa, a water goddess, was inside her right arm, ready to go on the offense at Abbie's command. Having those two artifacts become a part of her had effected a change in her, too. She had regained the confidence she lost after her friends in London died.

Together, the three of them could handle anything the Spell Gate market might throw their way. Best of all, they had Robert as a backup. The four of them waited and hoped the claw would grab them, too.

Nothing happened. All remained silent around them, with no claw in sight.

Abbie released a bitter sigh. "Guess we're not wanted." Most likely because she was a Grimm. "Jimi, do you sense the Spell Gate nearby?"

He leaned past the open window to look up and then sat back, shaking his head in sorrow.

"Never mind," she said in consolation. "Let's go back to that recital hall and see if the police have arrived there yet. At least we've now confirmed that the Spell Gate market and that hall are heavily involved in this mystery."

She reversed and sped out of the shopping center. When they arrived at the recital hall, two police units were on the street. Considering the crowds on the pavement, Abbie masked herself and the kids before they stepped out of the car.

"Shields up," she mentally told Arthur, and the ring's protection buzzed as it sealed around her. The kids already had the ring's protection as Nica wore her bracelets and Jimi carried his toy sword that Arthur used to connect to the kids.

She told both kids to not go anywhere inside the hall without checking with her first. Then, holding hands, they wove past curious unmasked pedestrians until they reached the line of officers keeping the throngs at bay. There, mention of Judith's name gained them a call. Soon Judith opened the front door and waved them past the police tape and up the central steps of the rectangular recital hall building.

A good thing, as rain sprinkled. That should clear the crowds. Abbie stepped inside the building and a shiver went through her, despite it being warmer and drier in here than outside.

Looking around at the shabby entryway, Abbie could easily believe this building had resisted Jimi's questions. It appeared to have lots of secrets to hide. Some might stretch back centuries if the old, worn wall hangings and hotel art were any indications.

She suspected that if it could have its way, this hall would have tossed them all out. Abbie squared her shoulders and stood her ground with her kids. "Any sign of children?"

"No," Judith replied, "but you'll want to see what we found." Judith squatted to be at eye level with Jimi before speaking to him. "You might help me make sense of what we found downstairs. Would you be willing to do that?"

Jimi nodded, eager to assist. "I want to find out who took River," he said in a determined voice.

"Brilliant." Judith stood and led the way.

They stepped past the entryway into an auditorium that sloped downward.

The last time Abbie came here with the kids to see a recital, the place had been so dark, she'd missed some details. Today, she noted how the place smelled stale and greasy and gave off a bad vibe. She wrinkled her nose, deciding never to come here again with her kids, not for a concert or any other reason. Some places were best avoided.

Muted lights shone from old-fashioned sconces as they headed down the right aisle covered in a green threadbare carpet. To their left were rows of ragged and stained red-upholstered seats and on the other side, a faded green, embossed wallpaper covered the wall.

"Where are your officers?" Abbie asked.

"Something magical is at play down below," Judith said. "Once I was told you'd arrived, I sent everyone out to do door-to-door checks in the neighborhood while we check out what's really in here."

They followed her through a door along a lonely corridor and then down a flight of narrow stairs and finally entered a large furnace room.

"Aside from the auditorium, the above floors house administrative offices," Judith said. "Most unused." She stopped when they reached the other end of the room.

Robert stared at the dirty white barrier, as if his butler had presented him with a silver tray containing an unwanted visitor's card. "You brought us here to show us a blank wall, Detective Constable Chan?"

"There's a door here," Judith said, walking to their right.

"But it's magically hidden. I've tried a few spells to open it, but whatever magic they used, it's strong."

"I'll check if someone occupies the room beyond," Robert said and walked through the wall.

"Oooh," Nica said. "Cool."

"Show off," Judith said with a grimace, but a moment later, Robert came flying out. Abbie and the kids jumped aside as he flew past and landed half into a boiler.

He picked himself up and came over. "Something in there does not want us to enter. There's an iron barrier that repelled me when I approached."

"Explains why my spells didn't work then," Judith said. At Abbie's questioning glance, she said, "Iron repels magic."

"I'll talk to it," Jimi offered and stepped up to lay his hand on the wall. He took Nica along, since his sister refused to release her hold of him.

"I was hoping he'd say that," Judith muttered.

The boy frowned at the wall. "Let me in."

Then he listened before he shouted. "Let me in!"

The wall shuddered as the building had earlier. Cracks formed along it. A section closest to them shifted, and the kids hurried back as, with a *boom*, the plaster broke apart, raising dust and debris as it fell away. As the air cleared, where once there had been a blank white wall, now stood an elaborately carved wooden door.

Judith knocked on it, causing a ringing sound. "May look like wood, but this is solid iron."

Jimi tried the doorknob and found it locked. He dramatically held up his arm and demanded, "Open sesame."

The door remained firmly shut.

"It's the iron, Jimi," Judith explained gently. "That metal is resistant to magical influence."

"My turn," Abbie said, stepping forward. "Where magic fails, let's see what a water goddess, even a demoted one, can do." She called on Hafgufa.

The cord within her arm made a noise that Abbie interpreted as a huffy, "Hmph," of contempt. Then the cord slithered out of her right forefinger and wrapped around the doorknob. Slowly, the cord squeezed.

The door vibrated as the goddess's influence flowed across the frame, repelling the iron. A keening sounded in the distance as if the hall itself screamed in agony from that touch.

"Kindly open this door," Abbie said. "Now."

The door swung outward, revealing a short, shattered corridor with debris on the floor. The short, littered passageway led to a dark room at the other end. Parts of the opposing walls of the corridor had broken and fallen in spots, revealing the magic-deadening iron within.

Robert nodded with admiration. "Now, that is notable."

Abbie retracted her cord, sensing Hafgufa's triumphant glow. Even goddesses had pride. One day, she hoped the goddess would share what had occurred in her past. After the London bombing, Abbie's psychologist had told her that talking about a traumatic event could ease the pain of it.

Jimi pulled away from his sister to head in first, but Judith forestalled him. "Allow me to go first, young man."

With a heavy sigh, he stepped aside, and Judith strode past him, carefully stepping over the rubble on the floor, her glowing baton in hand. Better than a Taser. Beyond the doorway corridor, she stepped into what appeared to be utter emptiness.

Abbie took Jimi and Nica's hands before following her friend into the other room, with Robert acting as rear guard. She shivered as she passed by the iron-embedded corridor walls, feeling a sense of oppression emanating from them. Her grip on the kids tightened until they reached the other side.

Someone had not wanted this chamber found.

Judith checked the wall for a light switch and, finding one, flicked it.

Fluorescent lights came on in flickers overhead, bathing the large rectangular space in a bright unflattering glare.

Holding onto her children with a fierce grip, Abbie squinted, waiting for her eyes to adjust to the change in illumination. She wrinkled her nose against the stench. The place reeked of fear and stale urine.

"Ew!" Nica said, pulling a disgusted face.

The room had stark white walls. Empty steel cages lined one wall, about a dozen. There was a working desk and chair pushed against the opposite wall in a corner. The cages had scattered rags, along with partially filled water bottles.

"That's River's." Jimi pulled out of Abbie's hold to race toward a cage in the middle of the rectangular room.

Abbie's cord shot out to wrap around his waist before he reached the cage bars and Robert appeared beside him, placing a restraining hand on his shoulder.

Nica ran toward her brother, while Abbie and Judith followed at a slower pace.

"Look," he said, pointing inside a cage when she and Judith arrived at his side. "Remember, Abbie? River wore this at school on Friday."

Robert retrieved the black hoodie with two fingers and held it up.

"It's his favorite jacket," Jimi said, his voice growing wobbly. "He wouldn't leave it behind unless he was in trouble. What's happened to him, Abbie?"

"I don't know," she replied in a calm tone. "The recital hall said he had been here," she told Judith. "This confirms it." She knelt and brought Jimi's face around so they could make eye contact. "What did we agree to in the car?"

Jimi's face flushed, and his lips firmed in a stubborn line. Then he looked down and said, "I'm not to do anything without checking with you first."

"That includes running into here," Abbie said.

"I'm sorry," he said, lip trembling.

She hugged him tightly, and Nica joined in the embrace. "These rules are to ensure that whatever has happened to River doesn't happen to you or Nica. Understand?"

He pulled back and nodded.

"If we don't stay safe, we can't help River," Abbie said. "Until we solve this case, you are not to go anywhere without me or trust anyone outside the SB crew or my family."

"Yes, Abbie," he said, finally looking truly repentant.

"Good." She withdrew the cord from around his waist and stepped aside.

Robert transferred the hoodie into one of Judith's tamper-proof evidence bags.

She sealed and labeled it.

"In breaking in here, we seem to have neutralized the room's magical protections," Judith said. "It should be safe now to have forensic check this over for DNA evidence."

She patted the boy's shoulder. "Good job spotting that jacket, Jimi. Don't worry, we'll find your friend." She gave Abbie a nod. "The police can take over from here. Shall we regroup at your place tonight?"

"Yes." Abbie checked her mobile. "We can have an SB meeting during dinner."

"Since the market leaves Earth tonight," Robert said, "Mr. Kanaan and Mrs. Irvine will return before then. They should have quite the tale about what they uncovered at the Spell Gate market."

"Do you think they're okay?" Jimi asked, sounding concerned.

"We will know soon enough," Robert said.

Jimi's reaction was to release a heavy sigh. So unlike her happy-go-lucky little man. She vowed to find River for him, if for no other reason than to see another of his endearing smiles again.

The evening meal was a quiet affair at St. Michael's cottage. All the Standard Bearers were present except for Yousef. He and Vivian had not yet returned, leaving the rest sober and worried.

They were well into their meal when someone knocked on the front door. Though that sounded more like loud *bangs* than respectful taps.

"Not Yousef's style of knocking," Talin said, glancing up from the tablet he'd been monitoring while eating.

"Whoever it is, made it past the house wards." Abbie stood to go check.

Robert accompanied her.

She'd recently refreshed her mother's

ward–magic-ingrained stones gifted to Grimms over the centuries. Once she touched them, they became a talkative lot, asking questions about whom to let in, whether they should blast intruders, or stun them. Were humans allowed in even if they gave off a threatening vibe? Were all supernatural beings forbidden entrance or only the ones Abbie disliked? And so on.

When Abbie queried her mother about her interactions with the stones, Margaret Grimshaw had given Abbie a worried glance. Then she admitted the stones had never spoken to her. Which was exactly what Abbie's Grandma Ruby had said about the Grimm artifacts she'd used.

Curious.

Once they reached the door, Robert cautioned Abbie to wait while he checked on their unexpected visitor. He easily slipped through the wood to do that. Being a ghost had its advantages. He returned to say it was a fellow he did not recognize. "Tall, dark-haired, and agitated."

"Whoever he is," Abbie said, "he's human or he wouldn't have made it past the wards." She also had an idea who it might be. After all, Yousef wasn't the only one missing tonight.

Chapter Five

Abbie opened the door to an athletic man dressed in blue jeans and a black shirt. She recognized him instantly, even though she had only met him once. Like his brother, he was memorable. This was Vivian's husband. A norm. "Good evening, Mr. Irvine. Won't you come in?"

"Sorry to disturb you," he said in a harried voice, lowering the hand he'd raised to knock again. He took a deep breath and said in a rush, "My wife hasn't returned. I'm concerned. Have you heard anything?"

"No," Abbie said. "We, too, are worried. We're discussing this case right now. Would you care to join us?"

"Yes, please," he said, looking thoroughly relieved to not have to face this crisis alone. As they headed to the kitchen, he added, "Call me Seamus."

"I'm Abbie. This is Robert."

Seamus started as Robert appeared beside him. "Right. The ghost. Viv mentioned you."

After making introductions in the kitchen, Abbie took her seat at the table and pointed to an empty seat beside Talin. "We're having fish and chips. Would you like some?"

"I can't stomach a bite. No offense. I'm sure it's delicious."

Judith came over with a plate of batter-fried fish and chips, anyway, along with utensils, and placed them before him. "Eat. This might be an all-nighter," she glanced at Nica and Jimi, before adding, "for some of us."

Talin fetched him a pale lager.

Seamus took a sip and stared broodingly at his plate.

They waited in silence. Within twenty-four hours, this man had lost his son, his brother, and now his wife. Abbie knew what torment that type of trauma could cause and empathized deeply.

Finally, Seamus took a chip and absently chewed on it as if he didn't realize he was eating after all. His frowning gaze wandered around the table until it paused when he reached Jimi. Then he teared up and searched in his coat pocket.

Abbie passed a tissue box from the counter to Talin, who placed it beside Seamus.

"Thank you." He blew his nose and then chewed on another chip. "I should never have trusted my brother with River," he finally said in a broken voice, as if even saying that hurt terribly.

Had he spent all day alone wrestling with that concept? Blaming himself for his son's disappearance and then his brother's death.

"Any brown sauce?" Seamus asked. "Tomato sauce?"

Abbie shifted the bottle toward him and he absently applied some to his plate.

"I knew something troubled him after the Olympic team dropped him," Seamus said, rapidly shoving chips into his mouth. "Only, I thought giving him a chance to do something useful, like taking care of River—whom he loved!—would give him something solid to focus on."

His pleading gaze met Abbie's. "We lost our parents years ago. I'm all he had for family. When we moved to Chipstead, he followed us here to be close."

"Why did you move here, Mr. Irvine?" Abbie asked.

His gaze became evasive. The straightforward question

petrified him. Odd.

"It was my wife's idea," Seamus finally said. "She... she thought this would be a good place to raise our boy." He gulped and focused on the lone fish now on his plate emptied of chips. He picked up his fork and knife and finished that off, too, within two bites.

Judith raised an eyebrow at Abbie, who passed over the plate of remaining batter-fried fish to Talin. He transferred two more to Seamus's plate, casually heating each to a steaming level during the transfer process. Then he shifted a caddy of condiments toward their guest.

"We never told Shane about River's abilities," Seamus said, taking a deep breath. "Once here, we emphasized to my boy to be careful not to talk about what he could do."

"He talked to me," Jimi piped up, holding his empty plate out to Talin. "But we swore not to tell anyone else."

Seamus's frantic gaze swung toward the boy and he released a shuddering breath. "Did he confide in Shane?"

Jimi nodded, digging into his newly delivered hot fish.

"Must have done it after we left," Seamus said in a sad tone, taking another tissue. "The boy can be impossibly impulsive." He chuckled. "It was Viv and my constant challenge about how to raise him. Life is hard for their kind. Yet, what we both love best about River is his adventurous soul. We want him to be a normal boy who is joyous, bold, and curious. Not a child encumbered by the fears, terrors, and repressions we inadvertently impose on him."

"Could your brother have mentioned River's ability to anyone else?" Abbie asked, trying to pin down a motive.

"He belongs to some private online chat groups," Seamus

said. "Shane liked to boast about his wins. After losing his place in the Olympics, I suppose he could have unwittingly boasted on there about having a special nephew instead. This is why we were so careful about keeping River's abilities a secret. Not careful enough, it's turned out."

"I've asked Goddess Aditi to watch over River," Nica said from beside her brother.

"Not Kali?" Abbie asked in surprise.

Nica shook her head. "Goddess Aditi loves children the most, so I prayed to her. She said River's angelic guardian requested an emissary watch over him until we find him."

There was profound silence in the room after that astonishing statement. Abbie finally asked, "Could you ask her where River is being held?"

"I already did," Nica replied, "but she said it's not her place to interfere or it would mess with River's karma. All his watcher can now do is to keep him safe for a little while."

"How long is a little while?" Seamus asked, wide-eyed.

Nica glanced at him and then took Jimi's hand before she met Abbie's gaze. "Not long. We must be quick, Abbie."

"Then let's get on with this case," Judith said, sitting up. "Seamus, did your brother have a laptop? We didn't find one when we searched his home and yours. When your wife gave her statement, she said she didn't know."

"He had a tablet," Seamus said. "It had his wallet. Contacts. Exercise schedules. His entire world."

Judith took out her notepad. "Who was his coach?"

"My wife said she'd given you those details."

"I'd like it again, please."

Seamus gave her a name.

"Did your brother always want to be in the Olympics?" Nica asked.

"He hoped to win gold," Seamus said. "I used to coach him when he was younger. Your age. Even then, I saw his potential. He had grace. Swam like a fish. Dove like a dolphin."

"Did he mention a recital hall in Sevenoaks?" Abbie asked.

"No. We only recently moved here and haven't had much time for attending entertainment events." He paused, fork halfway to his mouth. Then he set it down before making eye contact. "Why do you ask?"

Before Abbie could bring up their suspicions, Jimi blurted out, "We found River's jacket in a hall today. It was inside a cage in a hidden room."

Seamus instantly seemed to swell with hope and then his shoulders dropped as he deflated, saying, "Cage?"

"Yes," Abbie said. "We received a tip about the recital hall on Serpentine Road. When we arrived there, a man acting suspicious drove off and we gave chase."

"That carriage had two children," Robert said in a grave voice from beside the back door, where he stood guard. Before Seamus could ask, he added, "Not your son."

"He drove from that hall to a shopping center," Abbie continued, "and then we lost him at what we believe is the pickup point for the Spell Gate market. Some creature snatched that vehicle at the same spot where it grabbed your wife's car earlier today."

"Did you look inside the hall?" Seamus asked. "Is that where the cages were?"

"Yes," Judith confirmed. "We found River's jacket, but no River."

"That brings us to the Child Rescue Alerts," Talin said, pointing to his tablet. "Someone has hacked our system, issuing a score of posts in this region within the past twenty-four hours about missing children. It's crashing the system and overwhelming the helplines."

"Were you unable to identify the disruption's source, Mr. Higgins?" Robert asked.

"The culprits have erected a magical defense that's confounding me," Talin said. "I'm working on it. I'm close to circumventing the barrier."

"Why not tear it down?" Abbie asked. He'd proven last year that he could take down any computer system.

"It's extensive, with many moving parts," Talin said, his focus on his tablet. "If they realize I'm in, they might destroy all the juicy evidence to bring down whoever is behind this. I want to find the mastermind behind this ambitious plan, not merely the low-life hacker spreading disinformation."

He put away his tablet. "If you'll all excuse me, I'd like to get back to the Chipstead nick and carry on with this work. Also, Uncle Cal's still there, working alone, and it would be better if he had backup, even a distracted one."

Abbie understood his concern. She was certain Callum could take good care of himself, especially since Figg, the immortal's dog, shadowed him. But Talin had lost his aunt, and that wound was still raw. He wouldn't want to risk anything happening to his Uncle Cal.

"Make that two backups," Judith said, standing as well. "Let's bring some food for him."

"And for Figg," Abbie said absently, then caught herself. Why was she worried about the dog when she and Callum were feuding because he'd chosen to keep that killing mutt against her express wishes?

"The Recital Hall held no clues?" Seamus asked doggedly.

"Forensic collected fingerprints and DNA evidence," Judith said. "The lab results aren't back yet. I'll contact you as soon as I have anything concrete to release."

The two officers waved goodbye and hurried out.

Seamus sat back with a heavy, defeated sigh.

Abbie was happy to see his plate empty again. They'd been at their meal longer than usual because of their unexpected guest's arrival.

Eyeing her kids, she said, "It's past your bedtime."

"Oh," Seamus said, rising. "I should leave then. Thank you for that delightful meal. I must have been hungry after all."

"Stay," Abbie said, waving him back down. "I'd like us to talk a bit more. Robert can show you to the parlor and give you a nightcap while I settle the kids."

After washing up, she and the children headed upstairs. Once she had them in their beds, she sat beside Jimi. He was wide awake.

"We'll find River," she said in a forced confident tone, "and bring him home."

He stared at her in silence, eyes worried.

Nica sat up. "He doesn't believe you, Abbie."

"That's all right," Abbie said, tenderly brushing back Jimi's hair from his forehead. "When it's hard to believe in something, we have to have faith that it will work out anyway, even if it seems impossible. Can you both do that?"

Nica nodded.

Jimi stared at her in silence, lips pouty. Finally, he rose and hugged her tight, his arms wrapping around her neck. "I'm frightened," he whispered.

Abbie held him close, cherishing his soapy scent. "I know, love. Me, too. But we will picture River home soon, maybe even coming here for a playdate. Wouldn't that be nice?"

Nica scrambled across to Jimi's bed to get in on the loving. "Yes. I'll even play with him, even though he's little."

"Good," Abbie said, extending her arm to bring the little girl into her hold. "Now, go to sleep while imagining how good it will feel once River is home safe."

She kissed them goodnight, tucked both into their beds, shut off the overhead light, and left the room. She headed downstairs, determined that by the time the kids woke up, she'd either have more news about River's whereabouts or have a plan in place to get the boy home.

It could be because of Seamus's unexpected appearance tonight or Goddess Aditi's warning. Or even Yousef and Vivian's continued absence. Whatever the case, doing nothing tonight didn't sit well with Abbie. She had to do something.

Also, seeing children being taken in that vehicle by a villain who'd fled into the Spell Gate market had thoroughly upset her equilibrium. There were kids in danger and Abbie couldn't rest until every one of them was safely home with their families.

On the ground floor landing, she fished out her phone to call her mother to babysit her kids when the phone pinged. A text from Granny Chan asking if Abbie needed help. She was worried about Jimi's friend.

Deciding this might work out better, Abbie texted back before putting away her mobile.

She entered the living room to find Robert and Seamus

sitting side-by-side, deep in discussion.

Observing her sober expression, Robert asked, "Trouble?"

"Granny Chan's on her way over to watch the kids."

"Why? Are we going somewhere?"

She nodded and dropped onto the sofa. "We're returning to the recital hall for another look-see."

That wasn't a place she wanted to revisit, especially at night. Yet, her Grimm instincts, which were invariably accurate, clamored that she must return there. Now!

"Judith said that the forensic team had combed the place," Seamus reminded her.

"Yes," Abbie said. "I want to find what they missed." Her instincts gave another shove, but she resisted this one. Asking Seamus along on their midnight adventure seemed unwise. She didn't know him well. What if he was involved in this mystery? What if he were the perpetrator?

Except, when the villains took his son, Seamus had been out of the country and now seemed genuinely distressed that his wife and son were missing. Also, her ward stones had let him through the barrier around this house. They wouldn't have done so if he came with ill intentions or a supe in disguise.

Her Grimm instincts tugged again. Abbie trusted her internal guidance system. They had never led her wrong, though sometimes she didn't understand where they came from or where they planned to take her. A perilous way to live, true, but never boring. So, Abbie relented and said, "Seamus, want to tag along?"

Without hesitation, he was on his feet. "Let's go. It killed me to sit at home while Viv went looking for River. But she'd warned me to never enter the Spell Gate market. Said it would be tantamount to a death sentence for an unprotected human. Which is why tonight I came here instead."

The doorbell rang then. Could Granny Chan be here already? It should take a good half hour to drive here from Judith's home, and Abbie had only texted her a few minutes ago. The witch might have used a broom. Not that Abbie had ever witnessed Granny Chan flying one.

She hurried to the door, eager to start her nightly activity. Seamus was at her heels. Robert disappeared and was waiting by the front door when Abbie reached there.

He nodded to confirm Granny Chan was outside.

Judith's gran carried an overnight patterned carpetbag in one hand and a tiny rolled-up carpet tucked under the other arm, but no broom. "Evening, Abbie. Gentlemen."

"Thank you for coming on such short notice." Abbie gladly invited her inside. Must have flown here on her magic carpet. Having ridden both magical items, she was aware the carpet would be far more comfortable than riding a broom. "The kids are in bed, so they shouldn't cause you any bother."

"They never are," Granny Chan said. "Sweet little mites. Is Jimi fretting?"

"Yes," Abbie said. "I suspect he blames himself for River's absence. It could so easily have been Jimi that they took. We shouldn't be long. If you get hungry, I've put leftover fish and chips in the refrigerator."

"I don't eat after seven at night and I've brought a good book to read, dear. Watch your back."

Abbie, who was already out the door, turned back with concern. "Anything I should know about?"

"Look beneath what appears to be," Granny Chan said

cryptically. "Not all is ever what it seems." She gently shut the door before Abbie could ask any more questions.

"What does she mean by that?" Seamus asked, hurrying back to Abbie's side.

"No doubt we'll find out when we get to the hall." Abbie took a deep breath, grounding herself. It was a beautiful night to be out. The earlier rain had stopped. A balmy and brisk summer breeze blew through the garden. She sensed no demons lurking nearby. What more could a Grimm ask for?

"I'll follow you," Seamus said, pointing to his black Rover.

"Better if you come with us," Abbie said. "I'll drop you off here after we're done."

He hesitated and then nodded and followed her.

Robert was in Rosie's front passenger seat before Abbie and Seamus reached the car. Oh, to be a ghost and able to vanish and reappear wherever you pleased. Seamus took the back seat without the complaints Talin usually voiced when he was relegated to the rear.

"Why do you believe the police missed a lead?" Robert asked as they drove off.

"Instinct," Abbie said. "And Granny Chan confirmed it by suggesting we look under our feet."

"Literally?" Seamus asked, leaning forward to talk to them from between the two front seats.

"They could be another hidden space," Abbie said. "Might explain why no one was there when we showed up, despite us arriving unexpectedly."

"A hidden tunnel, perhaps?" Robert said.

"Crossed my mind." A familiar tingle at her nape suggested they'd brought along trouble. She met Robert's gaze and rolled her eyes. At his frown, she said in a loud voice, "Too bad Jimi's asleep in bed or we could ask him to help us find that tunnel."

"I'm here," a little voice shouted. Jimi pushed aside a dark covering and popped up from the boot. "I can help."

Seamus swung around with a yelp of surprise.

"Me, too!" Nica said, rising beside her brother.

"I'm taking you home." Abbie slowed and parked, allowing traffic to pass before attempting a U-Turn.

"We won't stay there," Jimi said. "We'll follow you."

Nica glanced at him and then at Abbie with concern. If her brother left the house, Abbie was certain, Nica would follow him. She sighed in resignation. She recalled being as willful as a child. At least Jimi wasn't trying to deceive her this time. He was telling her exactly how he planned to disobey.

"As always," Robert's voice whispered in her mind, *"they are safer with you than away from you."*

Abbie's mobile pinged.

The earl checked her phone that she'd attached to the dashboard. "Mrs. Chan says the children aren't in their beds."

Abbie gave Robert a fatalistic side glance. "Let her know they're safe with us and ask her to stay, in case Yousef or Vivian return tonight. Also, see if she can scry the location of the second hidden space at the recital hall."

"You're not seriously planning to take your kids with us?" Seamus asked from the back.

"I know this seems unorthodox," Abbie said, "but they are safe with me. They're not ordinary children."

"We're Standard Bearers," Nica piped in, and her brother solemnly nodded.

The kids scrambled over into the back seat and buckled

themselves in, Jimi sliding into his car seat without a grumble.

"We want to help find River," Nica explained, sliding in between Jimi's car seat and Seamus. "And Goddess Aditi said we could be of help if we're allowed."

River's dad didn't look happy with any of those explanations, but he clamped his mouth shut.

As a norm, he must find himself out of his depth.

"Seamus, could you and Robert monitor the kids?"

"Absolutely," Seamus said and Robert nodded.

Glad for that reassurance, Abbie turned her thoughts to this new goddess's suggestion about the kids joining in on this late-night hunt. Kali was more protective of these two, especially Nica. She wasn't certain about Aditi's agenda.

Abbie signaled and then pulled into the light traffic to continue on their way to the hall.

Kali had shown Abbie River's photo this spring, though, so finding the boy must somehow have divine repercussions. The enormity of that possibility was earthshaking.

"Indeed," Robert said in her head, as if he'd read her thoughts. *"I had not considered that angle."*

"Nica, was that all Goddess Aditi said?" Abbie asked.

Nica shook her head. "She also said that sometimes we must sacrifice for the greater good. I asked her what that meant, but she left without telling me."

Abbie wasn't happy with that answer. Another cryptic message, and not the good kind. She and Robert exchanged a worried glance, unnerved by the mention of a sacrifice.

Chapter Six

Abbie parked one street over from the hall. After they all exited Rosie, she bent to speak to the kids. "Remember what I said?"

"Follow your every order," Nica said.

"Jimi," Abbie said, "can you do that?"

"Ok," Jimi replied.

Nica took his hand. "I won't let go of him, I promise."

Abbie nodded, grateful for that big-sisterly gesture. "Good girl. Arthur, protection around all of us, please."

Her ring's barrier descended around the group.

Seamus started when the energy sparked on his mobile, tucked into his shirt pocket, and then swept over him.

"A little extra insurance to ensure we all come out of here in one piece tonight." She headed toward the hall.

Seamus followed her across the road, holding Nica's free hand, while Robert held onto Jimi. The children clung to each other. The sight released some of Abbie's lingering tension about bringing the kids along.

"Why didn't we park closer?" Seamus asked.

"The police are no doubt monitoring this place," she said. "I have a plan to enter that requires no one seeing us."

"Of course," he said, giving her an assessing glance. "My wife said you're resourceful and unpredictable."

"She did?" Abbie said, intrigued by his words as they made their way toward the hall while staying hidden behind bushes.

"Yes. She said that the word among the supe community is that you differ from other Grimms. Less lethal."

"What gave them that impression, sir?" Robert asked.

Seamus sent Abbie a sheepish look. "They won't admit it to your face, but all the supes in my wife's circle have been following your podcasts. Even her friends from Cornwall. She believes supes from all over England listen to you."

The news thrilled Abbie. It was the audience she wanted to reach with her specialized Grimm help.

Norms had the police, MI6, and countless other regulatory agencies they could turn to when in trouble. Supes existed outside that circle of protection.

When no supe ever commented, Abbie had wondered if she would ever earn their trust. Abbie's mother believed that witches had demonized Grimms over the ages. This news suggested Abbie's transformation from distrusted enemy to trusted ally had begun.

Vivian coming to her for help had been the supe community's first step in reaching out to a dreaded Grimm. It was now Abbie's turn to not only save Vivian's son, but bring her home safely as well.

At a hedge closest to the recital hall, she called a halt and pulled out her hand-mirror artifact. Time to see if Ruth could not only work for her, but her whole crew.

"What's that for?" Seamus asked, sounding curious. "An odd time to check your makeup."

Abbie swallowed her grin. "I hope it will help us gain entry into the hall without being seen. Seamus, we'll begin with you."

She held out the mirror and said, "Ruth, change Seamus's appearance so only we can see him."

The mirror flared. Seamus remained firmly in place with no visible change. Frowning, Abbie turned the hand mirror around to look into it. "Are you not able to do as I requested?"

"It's done," Ruth replied with complacency.

Frowning, this time, Abbie turned Ruth toward Seamus and looked into the mirror. He had no reflection. "Right," she said, grinning in delight, "we can see you, but no one else can."

She did the same procedure with everyone else, including herself. Before putting Ruth away, she told the mirror that from this point forward, if she tapped once, it meant turn invisibility on, and twice to turn it off. Ruth said she understood the signal and would comply.

They all headed to the back door at a faster clip now, no longer worried about being seen.

Abbie extended her right hand over the doorknob. "Be careful not to wake the hall," she warned Hafgufa, "or trigger any of its defenses."

The goddess's contempt vibrated along her arm, that Abbie felt a need to voice such a request. A slender golden light then extended from her right forefinger into the keyhole.

The lock clicked.

She gained entry into a large room that appeared to be used as a kitchen. She left the door open only slightly so it wouldn't alarm anyone watching the hall. They all slid in one by one. She quietly shut the door and locked it before they headed past the room.

"Let's go straight to the hidden door in the basement," she whispered. "This way."

They moved quickly from the kitchen to the front entryway. Abbie took the ramp down the auditorium's right side. She followed the path Judith had led her down before.

Once they entered the furnace room, they found the

hidden door wide open. She paused, holding a hand out to caution the others to be silent and listen.

From inside the kennel area, two people argued, and a child whimpered. Sounded like a little girl.

Abbie's pulse shot up. Could they have caught this group snatching another child?

She triggered her Grimm cord. *"I want to speak only to our party,"* she warned. Hafgufa often blasted her communications to anyone nearby.

Her cord showed she understood with a writhing inside Abbie's arm. The sensation came with an affronted sense of, *"I know who to invite into a conversation!"*

Hoping this would work, Abbie sent out her message. *"We're not leaving here without that child."*

"Yes!" Their affirming replies came in unison.

"Seamus, hang back here. You're the only human among us and you haven't the ability to defend yourself."

"I can swing a powerful right hook," he replied. *"And I'm now invisible."*

"Then, if anyone makes a run past Robert and me," she said, *"take your shot."*

"Roger that," he said with a resigned sigh. *"The children should stay with me, too."*

Abbie said, *"Agreed."*

"No!" Jimi said. *"I have my sword, and I will use it."*

Abbie had forgotten about that little extra protection Vivian had gifted him.

"If he goes in, so do I," Nica said. *"I won't let him go, Abbie. Ever."*

"Ever?" Jimi asked, sounding doubtful.

"No," Abbie said in a firm voice. *"Both of you will stay with Seamus."*

To her surprise, the kids' inevitable arguments didn't come. Jimi took Seamus's hand while Nica hung onto Jimi.

Satisfied, Abbie nodded to Robert before she headed toward the door. The room beyond that opening was dimly lit.

Looking in, she spotted two men arguing beside an open trapdoor at the far end of the room. From this side of the door, she couldn't see the cages, but guessed one of them must contain the girl.

She entered through the doorway, and something buzzed her. She had forgotten about the magic deadening iron.

Ahead, the men swung in her direction.

Abbie froze. The iron had broken Ruth's magical spell. She was visible. Also sensing her shield's absence, Abbie hurried into the room and said, *"Shields back up, Arthur."*

Her shield sprang up.

One man jumped into the trapdoor beside him. Abbie raced toward the remaining man, shooting out her cord. She caught him before he, too, could vanish down the hatch. The fiend she held wiggled to break free even as her cord squeezed him tighter.

"Look out!" a girl's voice shouted behind Abbie.

"Got him," Robert said, even before Abbie swung around. He held up a third fellow near the ceiling. He must have been out of her line of sight. His feet now swung in mid-air. The prisoner screamed, deafening them with his terrified cries.

"Silence," Robert growled and his captive gulped and shut his mouth.

Jimi ran into the room then, with Nica still holding his

hand.

Seamus was right behind them. “Sorry, Abbie,” he said, looking around furtively. “The boy pulled away as soon as the screaming started.”

Nica then ran toward a cage, pulling a reluctant Jimi with her. The lad seemed more interested in the trapdoor.

“I can’t open this door,” Nica called out, rattling the cage.

“Both of you stay with Seamus,” Abbie called back to the kids. “I’ll deal with that child in a minute.”

Her prisoner couldn’t possibly be human. Maybe he was a shifter because his body was freakily changing its weight where the cord confined him.

He shrank his top half as he tried to slip through the noose. He’d be free in a second if she wasn’t vigilant.

She ordered Hafgufa to restrain her prisoner’s spell-casting, and that finally stopped his squirming to escape.

Behind her, Jimi commanded, “Open!”

A lock clicked. A glance back showed the door of the cage that held the little girl swing out.

Nica leaned down to speak to the child wearing a frayed green polka-dot dress. “Don’t worry. Abbie will be here to help you in a minute.”

Jimi crouched beside his sister and laid his free hand on the floor and frowned with concentration.

Abbie suspected her one-track-minded boy was after the one who had escaped, possibly asking the hall where he went. Good. She wanted to know that, too. She glanced around, wondering what to do with her tiresome, shifting prisoner.

“Come back here,” Seamus shouted.

Abbie swung back to check if the little girl had run off, but it was her kids racing to the door, Jimi leading the way again. Still clinging to his hand, Nica met Abbie's gaze with worry, while Seamus ran after the kids.

"Jimi, stay here," Abbie called out in panic, but the stubborn boy raced out the door, dragging his sister along.

With Hafgufa restraining her prisoner, she was stuck here. If she released him, he'd flee the way his accomplice had through that trapdoor.

She shoved her captive into an empty cage, hoping a spell was on these kennels to keep talented little prisoners in place. Shutting and locking the door, she removed the key.

Robert did the same, sending his captive into a cage.

The little girl was creeping out of her prison and Abbie quickly locked the door. "Stay put. I'll be right back to help you. All right?"

She nodded and retreated into the corner of her cage.

Abbie's heart went out to this poor child, who looked terrified. She was no more than Nica's age, though she looked a lot thinner. Yet, she had no time to comfort her right now.

"Seamus, where are my kids headed?" she asked him, using her cord.

"Out front," came his instant response. *"Man, can they move!"*

Robert, having overheard that, vanished.

Good. He could cut the kids off faster than her or Seamus.

She speed-dialed Judith as she ran out of the hidden room, informing her about the two men they'd captured and the little girl they'd found. Then added that she and Seamus were chasing after Jimi and Nica, who might be after the third man who had fled down a hole in the hidden room. Abbie hung up before Judith could reply.

She was out of breath from sheer terror by the time she reached the entryway and ran out the front door into the quiet night air.

On the roadway, a dark hatchback backed up onto the street from beside the hall and screeched away, with Seamus racing after it.

Up the street, an unmarked car started up and Abbie prayed the vehicle belonged to police officers assigned to watch this place.

Her horrified glance returned to the fleeing vehicle's back window, where both her kids' heads showed for a moment before they ducked out of sight.

She was running after the car, wanting to send her cord after it, but soon realized it was out of reach. Then Robert appeared in the back seat. *Oh, thank God!* He glanced into the boot and then at her through the rear window.

His ghostly appearance gave her an idea. Abbie tapped Ruth once in her pocket, and said, "Over Nica and Jimi."

The mirror affirmed, "*Done,*" before the car turned a corner and Abbie lost sight of her kids.

"*Arthur, shields back up over the kids,*" she ordered her ring. The iron door would have stripped their shields, too, when the kids ran in and out of the kennel area.

"*Already done,*" came the ring's answer.

"*Thank you,*" she murmured, but her devastation at losing the children didn't lessen.

The unmarked car following the fleeting vehicle now flashed its lights. It was a police vehicle. Good. Though if the escaping car headed to the Spell Gate market, the police would be as helpless as Abbie had been the last time she chased a car to that shopping center.

Abbie used her cord to contact the kids and Robert, but neither answered.

"There is a magical barrier around the vehicle I cannot penetrate," Hafgufa said.

Abbie digested that devastating news. The fiend must have a spell around that hatchback.

The only saving grace in this terrible situation was that Abbie's kids had Robert with them. He wouldn't leave them.

Except, the source of his strength was St. Michael's, and, though he adored Nica and Jimi as much as she did,

Robert was tied to Abbie. Could he sustain himself inside that vehicle if the Spell Gate market snapped up the car the kids were in? Or would the gate's guardian spit him out, leaving her children with no protector?

Abbie shuddered in horror at her kids being drawn into that strange and dangerous market without her or Robert to guide and guard them.

Her chest squeezed tight, and she bent over, trying to draw in a breath. She felt as if she'd been stabbed through her heart. This must be how Jimi felt after they took River.

I'll get them back.

Then Abbie did what she'd advised her kids to do last night. She pictured them all sitting around the kitchen table enjoying breakfast tomorrow, laughing at one of Jimi's jokes.

Slowly, the tightness around her chest loosened, and she dragged in a lungful of air.

When Abbie straightened, Seamus was beside her, looking as devastated. This episode must have brought back the memory of losing his son. And then his wife.

"What the blue blazes do we do now?" he asked in a broken voice.

"We can't leave that child alone downstairs."

"Give me your keys. While you take care of her, I'll follow the one who took your kids."

"The police are already on his trail," Abbie reminded him, though it sorely tempted her to do as he asked.

Turning her back on her kids tore her apart. It was the hardest thing she'd ever had to force herself to do, but she returned inside the hall. "Chasing after the car would waste time, especially since you'd have to backtrack two streets."

"How many kids have to be taken before anyone does anything?" he shouted in frustration, following her.

"We need to try another tactic."

"Such as?" He kept pace with her agitated steps.

Now the air was filling her lungs, her brain ticked through her options a little faster and settled on one. The sooner she got those two men to talk, the sooner she could reunite with her kids.

Abbie's thoughts remained focused on Jimi as she tore through the auditorium.

What could he have been thinking about, to run away like that? How many times had she told him never to talk to strangers, certainly never to get into a stranger's car? Especially toward a man who had taken his friend. The moment she asked that, she knew the answer.

She should have guessed her boy would act this way. It was why he'd talked his sister into hiding in Abbie's car tonight. He was determined to rescue his friend and had guessed Abbie planned to do something tonight. Following this fleeing fellow was his way to get to River.

Jimi was naturally confident. Vivian's gift, however, could have given that natural self-assurance a gigantic boost.

Understanding Jimi's reasoning didn't come close to quelling her terror for her kids' safety. What Jimi didn't realize was that he was still a little boy. Also, his enemies could strip away his magic as easily as that iron doorway had shredded their invisibility spell.

"Maybe I should contact Kiros," she absently mumbled.

"Who's that?" Seamus asked, drawing Abbie's attention back to him.

Her Grimm instincts still had no qualms about Seamus, and Hafgufa seemed to trust him, so she said, "He's an immortal. I believe he and his siblings act as companions to the various beings they live among. To guide them."

"Like guardian angels?" Seamus asked.

Abbie glanced at him in surprise. Since learning she was a Grimm, she'd encountered many supes, and even a couple of goddesses and a fae queen. But no angels. "Do you believe guardian angels are real?"

"My wife is real," Seamus said, as he kept up with her speed. "So, why not angels?"

Why not, indeed. Believing in angels shouldn't feel any different from believing in supernatural creatures. Yet, it did.

"I don't know about angels," Abbie admitted. "Never met one. Fae, yes." They sped down the stairs. "Underwater creatures have helped me, and a demon once chased after me. So, I know those are real. Those two species also have a companion, immortal beings, created to guide them. Kiros is the humans' companion."

"Vivian's never mentioned companions," Seamus said, sounding as skeptical as Abbie was about angels.

Christianity was her mother's purview, one Abbie only half believed. Margaret Grimshaw had diligently taken her children to church every Sunday. Abbie's father had, however, encouraged his daughter to have a questioning mind. To deeply doubt what he'd labeled as "supernatural folderol."

Growing up, though she'd pretended to speak to ghosts and the angel at St. Michael's, she wasn't sure she'd believed they were real. The angel had never responded to her.

After Abbie spoke to Robert and then learned she was a Grimm, she was all in on believing in otherworldly events and supernatural beings. So, could angels be real, too? Beings whose sole purpose was to care for humans?

Her heart fluttered at the sudden touch of comfort the thought of angels brought. Silently, she prayed, *if my guardian angel is out there, I hope you're looking out for Robert, Jimi, Nica, River, Yousef, Vivian, and all the lost children.*

"Kiros helped me with a case last year," she said, shouldering her way into the furnace room and pelting toward the hidden room. "Not sure how much help he'll be now, as we have a disagreement we're working through and it's proving difficult to surmount."

For me.

She hurried through the door to the hidden room, feeling that magic-zapping buzz again. Seamus was right behind her.

They stopped short upon entering the kennel room, her chest heaving for air, and stared in dumbfounded silence.

The room was empty. There was no cowering little girl in

sight to comfort. No prisoners locked in cages to question.

The trapdoor on the floor was also missing. Not a mark hinted at where it had been.

"Cor blimey!" Seamus swore. "I should have stayed."

"They were magical," Abbie said in a hard voice, trying to absorb yet another painful roadblock to finding her kids. She'd hoped to get a lead from her prisoners about her kids' whereabouts. "What could you have done?"

"I could have slowed them," he snapped, turning his anger on her, "with my acerbic wit."

"Or they might have killed you," Abbie retorted. "How would that have helped rescue your wife and son or retrieve my kids and my friends?"

Even as Abbie instinctively struck back, she understood his rage, for it mirrored hers. They were both terrified. He was as desperate to find his son and wife as she was to find those she cared for. Tearing into each other didn't help either of them, though. Her thoughts scoured her mind for a solution.

"I wonder if Kiros could talk the market into refusing to take my kids in?" she mused.

"The immortal?" Seamus asked.

Abbie nodded. "Kiros is the one who could engineer such an extraordinary feat."

Chapter Seven

Abbie had avoided contacting Kiros since last summer. Even after he generously enlisted his oceanic sibling's help to retrieve a sunken ship as a favor to Abbie. She still refused to release her enmity against his diabolical underworld sibling.

Now her children were in danger, her calculations on that matter shifted. She pulled out her mobile.

Of all the Standard Bearers, Talin was the only one who had shown any compassion for Kiros. She suspected that they even went out for a cuppa now and then. While Kiros might ignore her, he would heed Talin's plea for help.

Talin didn't answer his phone, so Abbie used her cord.

"Yes?" he asked, sounding rushed.

At Seamus's startled glance, she guessed her cord was sharing this conversation with him. Just as well. He was a part of their case now.

"Please contact Kiros about the Spell Gate market," she said aloud. "There might be a supe-child-napping scheme being carried out from there. If so, I'd like his help to prevent the market from taking my kids. Or help me enter it."

"Will do," Talin said. *"Judith told me a police unit was in pursuit of the car with Jimi and Nica in it. Remain calm."*

"Right," she replied in a dead voice.

"I've broken through to the hacker," Talin continued. *"We're on our way there now. Will report back what we find."*

Ending her contact with Talin, Abbie headed to where the trapdoor had been, scanning the floor for its location.

She called on Hafgufa. *"I need you to crack open this hall's defenses."* Abbie laid her hand on the floor as she'd seen Jimi do earlier. "*Find me that hidden trapdoor.*"

The cord slid out of her finger and Seamus, who'd trailed behind her, gasped. Hafgufa slid across the floor, hither and thither, trying to sense where the opening lay. Then it paused and after a moment, turned liquid and sank into the concrete, slipping into the cracks' nooks and crannies.

The hall shook again as it had when Jimi yelled at it. The floor rose and Abbie jumped back as the trapdoor appeared and flipped open.

"Found you," Abbie said in triumph.

About to retract her cord, she instead sent it into the darkness of the hole. *"Hafgufa, is anyone down there?"*

"This tunnel is empty."

Abbie sighed at that bad news. But maybe she could follow where the escapees had gone. She retracted her cord and used her mobile's flashlight function to check down the hole.

Looked like a seven-foot drop. Hafgufa could levitate her up again if she needed out.

"Shall we?" she asked Seamus.

With a frazzled look, he ran his hand through his thick dark hair, and then he nodded.

Good enough. She sat on the edge, ready to leap down, when her mobile buzzed.

A text from Talin said the police unit that followed the fleeing car with Abbie's kids had ended the chase at the Sevenoaks Shopping Centre. They saw it park from a distance, but when they reached the spot, the car was nowhere in sight.

Abbie's stomach plummeted. The Spell Gate market had

snatched up Vivian and Yousef while they sat in their car in that shopping center. Chances were high that's what had happened to her kids, too.

With a shaky hand, she showed Seamus the text, more determined than ever to get into that market to recover all of their loved ones.

Arthur then notified her that his shields on the children had been severed. Ruth also gave her the same bad news. That meant the only protection her kids had was Robert, assuming he was still with them. Since he hadn't returned to her side, she hugged that thought to keep her sane and glanced again at her mobile.

Monday. Twenty past nine. The market would vanish from Kent in a little under three hours. All she wanted right now was to breach the Spell Gate market's barriers and find her kids and friends. She'd worry about how to get out again afterwards.

Why hadn't Kiros responded? She needed his help!

"Vivian said today is the last day the Spell Gate market would visit Earth this time around," Abbie said to Seamus, panic drumming in her chest. "If we don't get in by midnight, we may not find anyone until the market returns to Earth next, which could be a month away."

Catching his horrified gaze, she said, "I need to get in there tonight, Seamus." She debated abandoning following the escapees and heading straight for the shopping center now.

If Kiros didn't come through, she'd have to use her cord to breach the market. Before midnight. She'd rather be trapped in the marketplace with her kids than be stuck out here without them.

He shook his head, his gaze pleading with her to find

another solution. “You’re forbidden to enter, and Vivian told me never to go there. It’s unsafe for unmagical humans.”

“It’s unsafe for our kids,” Abbie said. “You don’t have to come, but I’m going. But even if I break in–big if–how would I locate our loved ones and then get out quickly? I need someone who knows how to navigate inside that magical marketplace and help me locate everyone.”

“Those who escaped from here could give us that info,” Seamus said, his thoughts running parallel to hers.

She leapt into the hole in the floor and barely rolled aside before Seamus landed beside her with a thump and grunt.

“You good?” she asked, rising and dusting herself down. The ground was raw soil.

“Yes,” he asked. “Which way did they go?”

Her flashlight highlighted an underground passageway. It stretched in three directions from this entry point. Having Jimi here would have helped decide which path their prisoners had taken. She would have to make an educated guess. The ground showed recent disturbances, most leading in one direction. “That way.”

The tunnel was tall enough to run through without either of them having to crouch. It swerved and twisted and finally came to an abrupt end.

Seamus came to a halt beside her. “Another secret doorway?”

“You catch on fast,” Abbie said, impressed by his quick assessment. The race through this tunnel also helped release her tension. She laid her hand on the nearest wall and asked Hafgufa to find the door.

It popped open above their heads.

Seamus put his hands together and offered to boost her.

"Thanks," she said, balancing her hands on his shoulders. He heaved her up. She caught the edge and levered herself up, with Seamus pushing her feet up from below. She rolled onto the pavement and lay still, taking a deep, grateful breath. The night air was cool. A glance around showed that she had arrived on a street.

A rat scurried by, squeaking in alarm.

"Nice to meet you, too," she said and stood. Not too many street lights. They'd driven by here on their way to the recital hall.

Seamus leapt up and caught the edge, before swinging himself gracefully upwards and landing lightly. "Where are we?"

She could see what must have drawn Vivian to this man. He could switch from awe to all business in one breath.

Before she could respond, a siren sounded nearby. A startling sound in the still night. The emergency vehicle was coming their way. She drew Seamus to the side of a building as police units turned the corner and sped down the street, straight toward them.

The vehicles stopped directly across from where they hid. Police constables wearing tactical vests over their uniforms swarmed out. Several circled an apartment building while the rest waited impatiently for a caretaker to allow them entry.

"Did you call them?" Seamus whispered.

"Not I," Abbie said and then spotted Talin and Judith exit from one vehicle.

"What are your friends doing here?" Seamus asked.

"They were supposed to be tracking down a hacker."

"If he's in there," Seamus said, pointing to the building across the street, "this could be the kidnappers' second base." He glanced at her with curiosity. "Why are we hiding instead of telling the police that?"

Abbie showed Seamus her mobile as she texted Talin. *What are you doing here?*

Where are u? he countered.

Abbie told him and, across the street, Talin swung around, but didn't spot her or Seamus in the darkness.

This is the hacker's last known location, Talin texted next. *U?*

Tracking down my escapees, Abbie responded. *Keep me posted.*

A man unlocked the building's front door and granted the police entry inside. Must be the caretaker.

Abbie put away her mobile and, with her now night-adjusted eyes, swept her gaze past the milling police cars to scan the surrounding area.

She nudged Seamus and then turned him in the right direction. "Does that look like a pair of skinny legs hiding among those bushes?"

"The girl from the cage?" he whispered, no doubt noticing the hint of a green dress. "What is she doing over there?"

"Let's go talk to her," Abbie said. "Wait," she said when he headed off.

He turned back with a frown of impatience. "What? Time's a-wastin'."

She tapped Ruth once. "Seamus and myself." A buzz indicated the mirror had activated. "Arthur, shields up over both of us, too." Once that sprang up, she nodded to Seamus. "Now we can see each other, but others can't see us, making it easier to circumvent the blockade on this street."

"Clever," he said, followed her with an appreciative grin. "Me like magic."

"Doesn't your wife use magic?" Abbie asked, chuckling.

"She is magic," he replied. "You have magical items that can be used on me. Big dif."

They made their cautious way across the street, past the flashing police units without being stopped. Their goal was to reach the large, many-limbed bush at the side of the building. They ducked under "Police Line Do Not Cross" tape cordoning off the public.

Seamus and Abbie then approached the bush from the far side. They soon recognized the young girl crouched within the branches as the same one who'd been in the hidden room.

"The poor wee soul is no doubt scared by people," Seamus whispered.

Abbie laid a finger to her lips to warn Seamus to remain silent as she inched closer, ducking under branches. She had her cord ready to catch the child. Finally ready, she tapped Ruth twice to take the invisibility spell down over her and Seamus.

The child jerked and scrambled to escape from them.

Abbie sent her Grimm cord after her. With any other cord, the wily child might have escaped. Hafgufa slithered in and around the branches to snag her victim around the ankle, above a pair of scuffed, black Mary Janes on her feet. No socks meant the cord could touch the child's skin.

The girl kicked and pushed, but the cord inevitably drew her toward Abbie.

The whole while, the child didn't cry out. If she had, the constables nearby would surely have heard. They were far enough away to be unnoticed in the dark, but a child's piercing scream could easily bridge that distance.

"Why isn't she screaming blue murder?" Seamus whispered behind Abbie. "I would, if something yanked me around by my ankle in the dead of night, outside, in a strange part of town. Or even inside my bedroom." He paused and then added, "Especially inside my bedroom."

"Don't know," Abbie said, wondering the same thing.

If she did scream, Abbie could use Hafgufa to silence her, but hoped she wouldn't have to. She didn't want to frighten this poor terrified child any more than she already had been by her abusers and now by Abbie's cord holding her.

Once she was closer, Abbie whispered, "I will not hurt you. Can we talk?"

The girl continued to squirm and Abbie whispered, "Please, stop."

The child cowered then, rolling into a ball and pulling herself as far from her captor as she could move.

She was petrifying this little mite. Abbie wanted to hug her and say she was safe. That no one would hurt her again.

As an EMT, she had seen her share of children react this way. Someone had traumatized this child. She needed to feel safe.

"Would you like me to take you to the police station?" Abbie asked.

The child shook her head vehemently.

Odd, but consistent with finding her hiding in the bushes when the police were right there on the street.

"All right," Abbie said. "How about we take you home, then? Would you tell us where you live?"

The child didn't react for a moment and then slowly, she shook her head.

Odd again. Yet, if someone had captured and kept this little one imprisoned, she might be too distressed to know what she wanted. She may no longer trust adults.

Time to take her out of herself and her problems. If Abbie could focus the girl's attention on a problem that was outside of herself, she might open up.

Keeping her voice as soothing as possible, she said, "I'm sorry to have frightened you. We're here because we need your help. A man from that hidden room has my son and daughter. I want them back."

It was hard to tell in the dark, but the child's shaking seemed less intense.

"You can't stay here, love," Abbie said. "It's unsafe for children to be out alone in the dark. Do you know of any place that you could go to? We can take you anywhere you want."

After a long moment of silence, the little girl sat up and Abbie finally got a good look at her. She would put her at about seven years old.

"Ten," Hafgufa said.

"Who said that?" the little girl asked, wide-eyed.

How could she possibly be ten? She was too skinny, too short, too everything. Nica was ten years old and a foot taller than this child and at least ten kilograms heavier, and Nica was light-weight for her age.

Of course, Nica had only put on more weight after Granny Chan moved into their cottage last year. The elderly witch had taught both kids how to cook all their favorite dishes and introduced them to a few new ones.

"My cord told us your age," Abbie said, finally answering the child's question. "It can talk to us." She tapped the side of her head. "In here."

"Oh, it's magic," the child said matter-of-factly.

"Yes," Abbie said.

If this little one was comfortable with the idea of magic, could she be a supe? That seemed to be whom these kidnappers targeted. "Are you ten years old?"

The girl shrugged. "I don't know."

Her answer was alarming. How long had they kept her?

"Thank you for warning me in the hall," Abbie said.

"He was going to hurt you," the child whispered, then slapped her hand across her mouth.

"It's all right," Abbie said in a reassuring voice. "No one will hurt you for telling me that. You don't have to go near any of those bad people again."

"But they're my family," she said in a teary voice.

Abbie and Seamus glanced at each other in concern.

"Crikey...," he whispered, "some families are odd."

"Do you have any other family?" Abbie finally asked.

The child shook her head. "Not since I was a baby."

"Who was your family when you were a baby?"

"I don't know. Zander says they left me and then died."

Hafgufa flashed a picture of a woman with red hair, a freckled nose, and round smiley cheeks. Rocking a toddler, she sang, *"Ba baa black sheep, have you any wool?"*

"Mummy," the child whispered in a reverential voice.

"Yes sir, yes sir, three bags full," Abbie softly sang.

The child's eyes fixed on her. Then she sang, "One for my master and one for my dame."

"One for the little boy who lives down the lane," Seamus added in his lilting Irish accent.

The girl chuckled. "You sing funny."

"Why don't we get out of here?" Abbie suggested, eager to head to the shopping center. Time was ticking on.

Maybe she could leave her with Talin and Judith.

"Could this child know where River is being held inside the Spell Gate market?" Seamus asked. "Your kids will be headed there, too, if they don't get caught first."

That possibility shoved turning in this girl clear out of Abbie's mind. But did she have time to grill her?

"I know where we can grab a bite to eat," Abbie said on a cheerful note, thinking there was a grocer at the Sevenoaks Shopping Centre. Judith could come to collect the girl there. "Would you like to go do that?"

The child's good humor died. "No!"

"Aren't you hungry?" Abbie asked. She looked half-starved.

The girl shook her head vehemently. "I'm not allowed."

At Abbie's silent, heartbroken stare, the girl explained patiently, "I was bad, you see. So, I can't eat right now."

Seamus drew in his breath as if to speak and Abbie laid a warning hand on his arm.

He was no doubt as upset by the child's words as Abbie. At least, the girl was talking and not struggling to escape. She took comfort from that. They had connected with her enough to get a response.

Her EMT training said—barring getting this child into the hands of authorities—her best option was to find a workaround for whatever mythology her captors had drilled into the child about these rules. For that, she needed information.

"How were you bad?" Abbie asked.

"I ran away," she said. "I can't eat now for two days. That's Zander's rule number four."

Seamus sucked in his breath while Abbie sat back on her heels, afraid to ask what rules number one through three might be. Who would order a child to not eat for two days?

"I see," Abbie said finally, on hearing how Zander controlled this child. "Well, rules are rules."

"Abbie!" Seamus said, unable to contain his horror.

"But," Abbie continued, "I'm a little hungry. How about you Seamus? You hungry?"

His frantic gaze flicked from her to the girl, and then he released a shuddering sigh and nodded. "Starving. I could eat a cow."

"Would you come with us, so Seamus and I can eat while we talk?" Abbie asked. "I want to hear about Zander and where he might be heading."

"I'm not allowed to talk to strangers," the little girl said. "Unless Zander asks me to." Her mouth turned down. "I also shouldn't have told you to 'look out.' That's two rules broken."

This child was better trained to follow orders than her kids. But if that meant Abbie was bringing up Jimi and Nica to be free and independent, even if they misbehaved occasionally and got into scrapes, so be it.

"I won't tell him," Abbie said.

"Me, either," Seamus said and crossed his heart.

"Thank you," the child whispered, sounding relieved.

"Also," Abbie added, "we're not strangers anymore."

"We're not?" the girl asked, glancing at her in surprise.

Abbie flashed her most disarming smile. "Not after we sang 'Ba Ba Black Sheep' together."

"Is that a rule?" the girl asked, frowning.

"It's our rule," Abbie said. "Isn't it Seamus?"

He nodded. "Yup. If we sing together, means we're friends for life and we can trust each other."

"Oh," the girl said, "I like that rule."

"We can sing the whole song while we drive," Abbie added and held out her hand. "Shall we go?"

The girl stared at Abbie's open palm for a long, pregnant moment. Then she glanced at the street where the police were still milling about. A coroner's van had joined the lineup of vehicles. That didn't bode well.

Chapter Eight

The growing chatter of bystanders was a good foil to keep her conversation with this child a secret.

"I'm not supposed to go with strangers either," the child whispered, "but I can't find Zander. He ran off first. His friends are in that building, but I don't know them. I followed them in there, but they frightened me. I need to find Zander."

"We can talk about how to find him, too," Abbie said, projecting briskness as she backed away, knowing her kids' had been hiding in Zander's car.

She dimmed her cord's glow to be less noticeable to passersby and stretched it so it wouldn't pull at the girl. Hopefully, the child would come of her own accord.

Abbie stood. "Let's go."

After a moment's hesitation, Seamus backed up out of the bush. They both waited in silence. Would the child follow them? Abbie needed this distressed girl to trust her. Quickly.

While she waited, she texted Talin again, sharing her screen's view with Seamus.

Found child. Taking her along to get more info on a "Zander." He might be lead kidnapper. U?

Found hacker murdered, Talin texted back. *Searching door-to-door for collaborators. No response from Kiros.*

She was digesting that last bitter pill when the child stuck her head out from within the branches. Abbie's breath whooshed out in relief.

Their trip back to her car took a while as Abbie had to work out exactly where she'd parked, compared to where they were now. Once they reached Rosie, she nodded to Seamus to get in the back and strapped the girl into the front passenger seat, noting she was skinnier than Nica.

Once in the driver's seat, Abbie reached into her glove compartment and pulled out three fresh blue paper masks. She passed Seamus and the child one each, and masked herself. As she drove away, she asked, "What's your name?"

The child didn't respond, fingering her mask.

"I'm Abbie Grimshaw. My kids' names are Nica and Jimi. Nica is about your age."

"You know Jimi!" the child said, sounding surprised. "Jimi Gill?"

Abbie glanced at her in surprise, and then met Seamus's stunned gaze in the mirror. "Yes, I'm his guardian. How do you know him?"

"Zander brought me here to talk to Jimi," the child said.

"Did he? Talk about what?"

"Not about, silly," the girl said and giggled. "Talk to. That's my job. To talk to special kids so they do what Zander wants them to do."

Abbie's glance swung to the little girl with grave concern as terrible thoughts flew through her mind before she returned her sight to the road ahead. Then, taking a breath to calm herself and her tone, she asked, "How do you do that?"

"I hold my hand like this." The child placed her hand across her throat. "Then I picture what I need someone to do and say, and I talk to them. Then the one I'm talking to does what I want them to do."

Abbie silently asked Arthur to strengthen his shield against magical assaults over both herself and Seamus. "Impressive," she responded. "And that works?"

"I'll show you." The child put her hand to her throat. "Abbie, sing."

The child's compulsion tugged at Abbie's vocal cords.

When she didn't sing, the girl said in a firmer tone, "Abbie, SING!"

The imperative, despite Arthur's protection, now had the drag of a tornado. This time, she played along and sang, "Ba baa black sheep, have you any wool?"

The child giggled and finished the next phrase, "Yes sir, yes sir, three bags full!"

Seamus's breath whooshed out in amazement. He wasn't alone.

The girl pointed to Abbie's face. "Why do you wear that?"

"Have you never worn a mask?" she asked.

The child shook her head.

"How about Zander?"

Again, a shake of her head. *No.*

Too young to be vaccinated, though Abbie had heard rumors that a vaccine for young children was being worked on.

England, and many other countries, had shut businesses because the COVID virus spread so rapidly. Only after they had a viable vaccine had places opened up this year. Was that why the Spell Gate market had come to Earth right now? Had they kept their gates shut to Earth while this virus spread like wildfire across the world?

She shook off that speculation. For now, she needed to find her kids, keep this girl safe from her abusers, and then she'd worry about the virus.

"I wear it for protection," Abbie said.

"From what?" the child asked.

"Did your family teach you about germs?" Seamus asked from the back seat.

The girl sent him a blank look, and he added, "Anyone ever tell you to wash your hands, even when it wasn't dirty?"

"No."

This was turning into a difficult discussion.

"Want to put that mask on?" Abbie asked. "Loop it around your ears."

"You have to turn it around." Seamus leaned forward and patiently helped her put it on correctly. "There. This hard piece goes over your nose. Now it won't feel so bad."

"Perfect," Abbie said, as Seamus sat back. "Now you're protected and safe from germs, too, just like us."

"I like being safe," the little girl said in a quiet voice. "You both make me feel safe."

"Good," Abbie said. "We won't ever hurt you."

"Zander says being hurt is how we learn right from wrong."

Abbie's chest tightened with fury, and Seamus's breath hissed out. In the mirror, he aimed his forefinger at an imaginary person and motioned to shoot. Zander, no doubt.

"Most of us are smart enough to learn without being hurt," Abbie said. "Zander may not have been smart enough to do that, but I bet you are. What do you think?"

The child's brows of deciding about a matter herself. Then she nodded and said in a daring voice, "Yes, I can learn without being hurt."

Abbie nodded her approval, choked up about having busted at least one of Zander's myths. They passed a streetlamp, and she noted how Seamus's eyes looked teary. She empathized.

She hated to imagine how many more myths had to be broken before this child would be free of this Zander.

They had crossed an intersection when the child pointed up the street. "There's one of Zander's friends."

Abbie instantly pulled over to the side of the road.

"Who did you see?" Seamus asked, rolling down his window and looking out.

The child was attempting to open her door, but had little luck because Abbie had locked up before they drove off. Also, afraid that at such an opportunity, the child might make a run for it, she had left Hafgufa wrapped around the girl's waist. The child might even have forgotten the cord was around her.

"Point out this friend," Abbie said, to distract her from wanting to leave.

"Over there," the child aimed a finger across the street toward a parked car. "The woman in the short blue dress."

The one she identified was getting into the passenger side of a Mini, parked across the street next to a music shop

Abbie made note of the vehicle's number plate.

When the car pulled out onto the street, she tossed her mobile to Seamus and said, "Please check my phone contacts for Judith. I need to let her know I'm leaving town tonight."

"Where are you going?" the girl asked as Abbie pulled into the street. After a pause, she added, "May I come?"

"Do you want to?" Abbie asked, surprised. She may not want what Abbie had planned, which was to hand her over to Judith, but why would she want to come with her? "Don't you have to go back to Zander?"

The phone rang then, and Judith answered before the child replied. "Abbie, what's up?"

Seamus held the phone up to Abbie.

"I need you to follow a car with this number plate." Abbie gave the details she'd noted. She then told her where that vehicle had parked and where the Mini was headed. The police could track down Zander's friend with that information.

"Got it," Talin responded. He must still be with Judith.

She continued driving toward the shopping center. It should be around the corner.

"Any luck at the hacker's place?" Abbie asked.

"They knew we were onto their scheme. Not only did they kill the hacker, but they also cleaned out the place."

She glanced at the little girl, who now held up a finger pointed to her head.

"Was he shot in his forehead?" Abbie asked.

"Yes," Talin said. "How did you know?"

Abbie paused a moment to gather her thoughts. They'd found the child outside the building. She'd told Abbie that she'd followed the fleeing men inside, and they'd frightened her. Now she had an idea what could have happened. "I might have a witness."

Beside her, Seamus nodded, as if he'd come to the same conclusion.

"What witness?" Talin asked.

"A smart little girl." Abbie winked at the child, whose eyes widened as if Abbie had surprised her.

She checked the mobile clock. Ten thirty. Time was running out.

"Bring her to the Chipstead nick," Judith said.

No, was Abbie's immediate thought. She needed to get into the Spell Gate market. Now.

The child's earlier admission about her compulsion talent had given Abbie an idea. A dodgy one, but one that could help her not only enter the market, but find her kids.

Also, she and this child had formed a tenuous connection. This girl trusted Abbie, to a degree. Which meant she had an opening to break whatever insidious hold Zander had on the girl. For that, she needed more time with her. That was surely worth taking a risk or two. On everyone's part.

This extraordinary situation also required a bold move. And a brief period in which to do it.

She took the next turn and stepped on the gas pedal.

"Abbie?" Judith said. "Where are you?"

"We're on our way to the Spell Gate market," Abbie said. A glance in the mirror showed Seamus start at that.

Her friends on the phone were silent.

Finally, Judith said, "Is that wise? Or even possible?"

"Yeah, I thought the Spell Gate wouldn't let you in," Talin added, sounding wary.

"I have someone here who can help me with that little problem. Someone who might be as persuasive as Jimi. Who I hope will help me." Abbie glanced at the child, who nodded her head.

Promising. Relief flooded through her. This might work, after all.

"Who is this child?" Judith asked. "One of the missing children?"

"No." Abbie glanced at the child. "At least, not recently. Please tell the nice lady on the phone your name."

The girl hesitated and then, when Seamus held the phone closer to the child, she said, "Emily."

"Emily Bryant," Abbie's cord clarified.

"Did everyone hear that?" Abbie asked.

The child frowned. "That sounds familiar. Is that my full name?"

"Yes," Abbie said. "The cord's never wrong."

"We heard, too," Talin confirmed.

Abbie drove into the shopping center's car park then and an enormous weight lifted off her shoulder–her Grimm senses telling her this was the right move.

As expected, it was mostly empty at night, but for an occasional parked vehicle. She stopped where she'd seen Vivian and Yousef's vehicle being taken by the gate.

She waited a moment to see if the Spell Gate would take her. The seconds ticked by and nothing happened. No doubt because she was a Grimm and there was a norm in here. She sighed in resignation. We'll do it the hard way, then.

"Hafgufa, show everyone I'm talking to what Emily's mother looked like the last time Emily was with her," Abbie said. Her cord instantly shared the vision of the freckled-faced mother singing to the little girl. They must have snatched this child shortly after that precious moment.

"Everyone see that?" Abbie asked.

Emily nodded and Talin and Judith said, "Yes."

"Check your past alerts for a missing child that looks like that little girl and her mother." Then, focusing on Hafgufa, she asked, *"How long ago is that vision from?"*

"Four years, three months, and eight days ago."

Such a long time to be kept captive. Poor little mite. If all went well, Abbie would have Emily back with her mother soon, and her kids and River back in their respective homes.

"And Talin," Abbie said, "brush up on Stockholm syndrome. We'll need your special healing help with that once we return home."

Talin could help the girl release any negative emotional energies within her. After his success with Mama D'leau, he had become quite adept at using his energetic wizardry on more than electronic systems. He could now help people with their pent-up energies causing emotional distress.

Talin had told her he'd been practicing on fellow officers in his spare time and becoming quite popular at the Chipstead nick.

"Now, say goodbye, Emily," Abbie said.

Talin hurriedly said, "No, wait!"

"What?" she asked.

"I spoke to Kiros."

"And?"

"He refuses to help–" he paused "–unless you agree to make peace with all of his siblings."

An answer Abbie had half expected, but it still felt devastating to have it confirmed. Now the time for a decision had arrived, she still resisted making a peace pact with Kiros's underworld brother, Vulcan. He'd killed her friends and countless Grimms.

She shook off her disappointment. A new option for getting into the magical market had opened up that she hadn't had when she desperately asked Talin to contact Kiros.

Emily was a safer choice. At least, she hoped so.

"He also warned you to stay away from the Spell Gate market," Talin continued. "It's a sensitive port, as it's the one place where we can bypass the rule about no interaction between different realms. So, they charged one of their siblings with its security."

"Which one?" Abbie asked. *Please don't say it's the murderer.*

"Tuuli, the fae companion. Kiros is also certain you're mistaken about children being taken into the market against their will or Tuuli would know about it. Nothing happens in the market without her knowledge and she's diligent about reporting to them. It was a requirement of the job when they put her in charge."

Now that was helpful information. She'd never met Tuuli, but the fae loved to bargain. Abbie had been of help to a musical fae queen in the past. Could she use that connection to convince Tuuli to assist with her dilemma of getting her family and friends back?

Worth a try.

"Tell Kiros that he should reconsider his position," Abbie said. "Children's lives are at stake." She then waved her hand in a goodbye gesture.

"Bye," Emily said, and Seamus hung up before handing the phone back to Abbie.

"Thank you." She re-attached her mobile to the dashboard. No turning back now.

"I believe Zander has returned to the Spell Gate market," Abbie told Emily. "I plan to follow him. Do you still want to come with me?"

"Yes," the child said, though she sounded hesitant, which made Abbie wonder if she'd been mistaken in thinking Emily would help her get into the Spell Gate market. Her gaze flicked to her mobile. In less than an hour, at midnight, the market would transit out of Earth, and her opportunity to get in would slam shut.

"I'm not supposed to enter the market," Seamus repeated in a grave tone, and slumped back into his seat.

She met his gaze in the mirror.

"Vivian said it was unsafe for humans and, before she left, she made me promise never to go in there. Not even to help her."

Abbie's Grimm senses said there was a clash between what he said and how he felt. Despite all his wife's warnings, Seamus wanted to go to the market to rescue his loved ones. She saw the struggle in his conflicted gaze and sympathized. She'd do anything the same, even risk her life. As she planned to do now.

"Zander will be angry that I ran away," Emily said into the silence, her voice trembling.

"I could talk to him," Abbie said. "Explain how I used my cord to make you come. Then he'll know you didn't run away."

"Oh, that's good," she said, relieved. "That means I can eat."

"Yay!" Abbie said, her heart breaking at this tormented child's life.

Seamus sat up with a determined look. "If Emily dares to face her Zander, I can certainly face my wife's wrath. I'm coming with you!"

"Yay!" Emily said.

Abbie wasn't as thrilled by Seamus's decision, but there was little time left to argue the matter. She needed to bring home her kids, River, his mother, Yousef, and Robert. She glanced at Emily. And this child, too. Listing them all made this feel like such a daunting mission. It would help to have Seamus along to help her find her missing friends, but Vivian had wanted to protect her husband.

She took a deep, shuddering breath at what she was about to attempt. Her mind took her back to her childhood days when she used to visit St. Michael's church and talk to the angel in that old stained-glass window.

As she had back then, Abbie whispered her worries to the angel. She sensed her listening as she used to imagine she did back then. But like in the past, the angel didn't respond.

With a sigh of regret, she did what Nica often did, what her mother had taught Abbie to do at bedtime. She put her hands together in prayer. *Please help me retrieve Jimi and Nica and my friends, but help me do that without endangering Seamus. Oh, and to reunite Emily with her mother.*

It was a childhood ritual that came easily. Her father would have shaken his head at her foolishness, but Abbie was unwilling to leave any stone unturned to save those she loved.

"What are you doing?" Emily asked.

"Praying." Abbie glanced at the child and then checked her mobile. Thirty minutes to midnight.

"How about we take some snacks with us?" Abbie asked Emily and Seamus.

"Zander only feeds us kids his special porridge," Emily said.

"What's that?" she asked in concern. It didn't sound nutritious.

Emily shrugged. "Porridge mixed with a special powder that he says keeps us alive."

Abbie had to gulp at that terrifying admission. Was he drugging these children with a magical potion?

Even if Emily couldn't remember eating anything but this doctored porridge, she must have once had parents who fed her what she loved. "Hafgufa, what did Emily like to eat?"

"Crisps and a fizzy drink."

"Oh, yes," Emily cried. "I'd forgotten I love that!"

Abbie glanced over her shoulder at Seamus.

"Do we have time for this?" he asked.

"I just checked. We have an hour," she said, the lie flowing out of her mouth with surprising ease. "We'll make it if you're quick about it," Abbie added. She then gave him the right incentive to breach his fatherly defenses. "Emily probably hasn't eaten in ages."

"I can grab a few things from that grocer over there." He was already half out of the car.

"What kind of drink?" he asked before shutting the door.

"Cola," Emily said.

"Same," Abbie replied, her heart breaking at deceiving him. He'd been such a help to her tonight.

"I'll be quick as a bunny," he said and hurried away.

Chapter Nine

Abbie watched him leave with sadness and then checked her mobile. Time to make her move.

She removed her mask, tucking the material into her pocket, and had Emily do the same. They were unlikely to need face coverings where they were going. Because she was emergency personnel, they vaccinated her for COVID.

Belatedly, she wondered if she might inadvertently carry virus particles through the gate. To be on the safe side, she pulled out a sanitizer. After using a spritz on her hands, she asked the child to do the same. "Emily, have you ever spoken to the Spell Gate portal gatekeeper?"

The child shook her head. "That was Zander's job."

"Do you suppose you could convince the gatekeeper to allow me through along with you using your talent?"

"Without Seamus?" Emily asked, glancing out the window toward the grocer.

"Yes. The market leaves Kent in a few minutes and we'll miss it if we don't try now."

"Okay." Emily shut her eyes and put her hand to her throat. "Spell Gate, we need to go through now."

Abbie leaned out her open window and glanced up. Her chest was tight. She deliberately forced herself to take a calming breath.

Nothing changed overhead. All remained dark and still. A cool wind brushed against her skin, ruffling her hair. Had she waited too long?

"Try again," Abbie said. "Picture us going through and be

firm."

"Spell Gate!" Emily scrunched her eyes shut, one hand on her throat, and one fist placed on her hip. "Open up and let us through. Now!"

The car shuddered.

Abbie leaned away in the nick of time as sharp claws swung in through the open window to grip the roof. Still, the vehicle remained where it was.

Deciding the gate needed a nudge, Abbie sent Hafgufa up to the closest claw. The slender golden thread gripped the claw and the entire vehicle shuddered again and her cord sent her a flood of images.

Centuries of patrons traveling through this portal appeared in her thoughts. It was like reading Klaus. The moment that thought occurred, the heavy book landed on her lap.

"Klaus, go home," Abbie mind-spoke to the book. *"I don't need you right now and you're too big to take along."*

The book instantly shrank into a miniature version.

Rolling her eyes at the obstinate tome, Abbie tucked the now tiny version of Klaus into her bra.

Meanwhile, Hafgufa continued to inundate her with images. The Spell Gate opened and closed, the portal expanding or shrinking to accommodate the size of its patrons. Humans, watery beasts, fae creatures, demons, and even whole celestial bodies passed through that amazing portal.

"Wow," Emily said. "This is so cool."

She checked on the child and noticed her pupil flickering. Her cord was transmitting the same images to both of them. Great. At least, that distraction ensured Emily missed Klaus's unexpected arrival.

She was glad about that. The Grimm Tales was not a book she wanted to advertise widely. It was one Grimm gift about which she was super protective. It housed too many family secrets.

"No!" Seamus shouted before his running footsteps pounded on the pavement. "Wait for me!"

A scream drew her attention in time to see Seamus being flung away for daring to approach. Abbie shuddered, holding her breath until he got up, holding his head. Thank heavens he was okay.

The images abruptly stopped. Her view of Seamus, the scattered bag of food he'd been carrying, and the entire mall was gone. She found herself in a dark, silent landscape. Something shifted. A circular opening appeared ahead. It took on the appearance of an eye with a bronze pupil. Was this the gatekeeper?

Then another movement drew her attention to her side, where a being of light approached through the darkness. It was so bright, Abbie had to squint, having a difficult time looking at it directly.

This being emitted a sense of immenseness, grandeur, and limitless power. If she didn't know better, she might have thought she was in the presence of a god. She half expected a host of angels to sing.

Except, something felt wrong about this light being. Her Grimm instincts said this was a creature to beware. Abbie instinctively sent that warning toward the bronze eye.

That gaze swung toward her with surprise.

"That is a Grimm," the light being said in a tone of utter

disdain. "I was warned she was coming. You must deny her entry and send her packing!"

Someone had warned this being about Abbie's arrival? Who? The only ones who knew of her wish to enter the Spell Gate market were her SB crew and Seamus. And Kiros! Did that mean this was his sister, Tuuli? Talin had said she was in charge of market security.

Abbie had asked for Kiros's help to her get into the market. Had he, instead, sent his sister to keep Abbie out? She'd have a thing or two to say to him about this when she returned home.

The bronze gaze swung from the speaker to Abbie.

"This light being is not your master," Abbie said, making her words loud and crystal clear. "You are not beholden to it and you do not have to obey its command." She hoped that was true. "Make up your own mind about me."

Whatever the veracity of her words, she had captured the bronze gaze's attention.

Little fingers slipped into Abbie's hand, and she realized Emily was with her. Was she frightened? She clasped the girl's hand in comfort. Then support flowed in from their hold. Emily wasn't afraid, she was helping.

Bolstered by that vote of support and compulsive power, Abbie held firm to the child and said, "Spell Gate, you are not under anyone's authority." This time, her words came out loud, layered with vibrational authority and compulsion. Emily's doing? "You know what to guard against. So, decide. Am I the one you should be wary of?"

The gatekeeper's glance stayed on Abbie and then it pushed back, not against her, but against the compulsion spell Emily exerted.

The child gasped and dropped her hand from her throat.

So, spells couldn't work on this aperture. Made sense. A being that guarded a portal where magic was the currency had to remain incorruptible by powerful forces.

As if sensing she had won her point, Tuuli commanded, "Send the Grimm away!"

The stark order startled Abbie. Could Tuuli also have a compulsion talent? Is that why she thought she had dominion over the Spell Gate, even after this portal had rejected a control being placed on it?

Emily tugged at her hand, reminding Abbie they had to get through this gate.

"My children and in the market and I need to retrieve them," Abbie said to the gatekeeper, deciding that truth was all she had left to work with. "Their mother trusted me to watch over them, and I promised her I would."

The gatekeeper, who had been observing Tuuli with an icy stare, now swerved its attention back to Abbie.

"I love them, you see," she said, her voice cracking. Until she admitted it aloud, pleading for a chance to save Jimi and Nica, she hadn't realized how true that was.

Since the bombing, Abbie had shielded herself against the pain of losing those she loved. Even as she made new friends, and grew closer to the kids she took in, she'd failed to comprehend how deeply she'd come to care for them all.

Last year, after releasing that fear of losing her loved ones, her immense ability to love must have also come out to play. As a child, it was this facility to care without inhibition that had made her befriend all those buried at St. Michael's graveyard. That childish, open heart was no longer willing to cower, to stay hidden.

For months now, it had been bubbling up, wanting to embrace the entire world. Was that why she'd instantly attached to Emily and wanted to protect her? The sensible act would have been to hand her over to Judith. Very possible.

As much as her open admission of her immense love for her children had opened Abbie's eyes, it seemed to resonate with the gatekeeper, too.

For it *blinked*, physically and metaphorically. There was no other way to describe the gate's reaction to her impassioned words.

Then Abbie felt her car being lifted and flung across the cosmos. She shut her eyes, quelling a scream of terror. Was she being evicted from the gate? Had she lost this battle? If so, Emily would pay the price along with her.

She yelled at Arthur to raise his shields to full strength and opened her eyes, wanting to see their fate.

Rosie flew across a barren landscape. They were no longer near the blackness of the gate, nor anywhere near the shopping center's car park. It was also now daylight, though she couldn't spot the sun anywhere on the horizon.

"We've arrived!" Emily cried. "It worked," the child said, bouncing in her seat in excitement. "The gate listened to me and let us pass through."

Abbie didn't dissuade her, but she suspected the gatekeeper had made up its own mind about allowing them entry. It hadn't allowed either Emily or Tuuli to decide on its behalf. That must have displeased the fae companion. Now she would have to use other means to deal with Abbie.

Something to keep in mind while she was here. She silently

said to Arthur, Hafgufa, and Klaus, *Stay on guard!*

All three gave silent vibrational acknowledgment that they'd heard her request.

The car, still moving, suddenly tipped downward. She stomped on her brake, but that had no effect. Not surprising since, aside from their magical flying, the car key was still in her pocket. Before Abbie could ask Arthur to cushion their landing, they hit the ground, bouncing a few times. Their seat belts kept her and Emily from being knocked senseless.

The car skidded forward, sending up a dust flare before it finally came to a stop.

Once the dust settled, Abbie had a better look around. Ahead, a "make-do" car park had formed from rows of lined-up vehicles, as if people had driven here to attend a summer concert. Except, these were not all cars.

Oddly shaped three-wheeled contraptions sat beside vehicles with wings or sails. One looked like a globe.

She turned on Rosie's engine and drove until she found an empty spot. She slid into it beside a vehicle on one side that looked like a fish tank with a tiny multi-limbed beast. On the other side was a flying carriage, which stayed suspended a few feet above the ground.

Abbie released a sigh of relief, thrilled to be one step closer to finding her kids and friends. She glanced at Emily with a smug grin. "Who wants to go to the market?"

"I do," Emily said, but sounded thoughtful rather than excited. "You'll like it there," the child added. "They have loads of food. I'd like to try some, too."

"Good idea, since we missed out on the crisps." Unbuckling, Abbie exited Rosie beside the fish tank, with the creature inside watching her with avid interest. A sign on the bottom had scribbles on it. She laid her right hand on the sign and Hafgufa translated the words to *Beware, this baby bites.*

Abbie pulled her hand back and slid sideways until she was past the tank.

"Arthur, can you sense Nica and Jimi?" she mind-spoke to her ring.

The ring gave her an unhappy buzz.

She then asked her cord to contact any of their missing loved ones.

Hafgufa offered her a similar negative answer.

Resigned, Abbie headed toward the market's entryway. Ahead, two giant marble griffins, their wings half-extended, sat on opposing pedestals guarding the entrance.

A lone, dark-haired man dressed in Bermuda shorts, a polo shirt, and a black Cordoba hat questioned patrons wanting to cross into the market. There was no lineup as traffic flowed into the market without a hiccup.

Must be a straightforward job since the Spell Gate only allowed anyone into this realm who had the authority to come. Also, this mustached guard was likely magical.

"Halt," the guard said, with a strong Spanish accent, his focus on a stiff sheet he held.

Abbie stopped, pulling Emily closer.

"We're here to attend the market," she said in an assured tone, as if she came here every other day. Standing straight, shoulders back, she gazed directly at the guard.

"Supe child," the guard read, before he flicked a glance at Emily. "Check."

He glanced at his sheet again and swallowed. "You're a

Grimm!" As soon as he said the words, his gaze flew up toward Abbie. "How did you get in, *señorita*?"

"The gatekeeper allowed my entry," Abbie said. "How else could I be here?"

"But the market forbids your kind," he stuttered.

"Yet, here I am," Abbie said in a reasonable tone. "The rule barring me must have changed." She pointed to his sheet. "I'm on your list, aren't I?"

He glanced at his listing, his hand trembling so much, she doubted he could read it anymore. Then back up at her. "*Sí*, you are. The gatekeeper updates this before anyone arrives."

"Must be official then," she said.

"Have you been here before?" he asked, voice now shaky. At her patient stare, he added, "Of course not. Well, there are other rules." He frowned at her and cleared his throat. "You must not break those."

"What are they?" Abbie asked.

"Circle," he called, and a white lighted circle, similar to a small hula-hoop, zipped forward to stop a few inches off the ground on the market side. Pointing to it, he said, "You are to stay within that circle the entire time you are in the market. It is your only means of safe transport. Understand?"

Abbie nodded. "Circle. Transport unit. Got it." How cool. A magical rideshare service. "How does it work?"

"You step inside it and tell it where to take you. It will carry you to anywhere or to any stall you wish to visit or to anyone's side. No stepping out of the circle. Ever."

"No stepping out," Abbie repeated, thoroughly pleased with this arrangement. If she said she wanted to go where Nica and Jimi were, would the circle take them there? She could hardly wait to find out.

Past the guard, the market looked like an ordinary place, despite its magical reputation. Vendors at open booths hawked their wares. She spotted pretty scarves and vases in nearby stalls. Even elaborately woven rugs. Could they be flying ones, like Granny Chan's?

"Is that circle for both of us?" she asked.

"Both. The circle will be under your total control."

She took a deep calming breath in and got a whiff of the appetizing scents of exotic foods from the market. She could hardly wait to get started.

The guard looked her up and down. "Folks bargain for what they want in the market. Do you have anything to bargain with?"

"Does it have to be magical?" she asked.

"Of course."

She shook her head, unwilling to bargain away the only unattached magical artifacts she had on her–Ruth, her mirror, and Klaus. "Does this mean that if Emily needs a bite to eat, we won't be able to buy food?"

Under his breath, he muttered, "*Turistas*." Then, fishing in his pocket, he pulled out three stones. After rolling them on his palm, he picked the smallest, a pretty azure one, and offered it to her. "You can exchange that for food."

"I appreciate this," she said. What a kind man.

Abbie examined the stone. A charm on it tingled and sparked against her fingers. Round and smooth, it reminded her of her Grimm wish bombs that Jimi loved. Those were bigger, twice the size of this tiny blue orb, and extremely dangerous.

"What is this stone?" she asked him.

"A wish maker."

That made sense. Her wish bombs acted similarly, reacting to stated needs.

Abbie glanced with speculation at the guard. Where her cord and ring had failed to connect to Jimi and Nica, this guard could likely confirm if they went past him.

"Did a boy come through here recently?" She held her hand up, palm down. "This tall, black hair, brown face, talks to things. He would have been with his sister. She's a little taller than Emily." She added a description of their clothing.

"*Sí,* went through earlier," the guard said. "Came in shortly after Zander. Thought they were his usual haul of magical kids. Except, instead of walking with him, they were following a good distance behind. They also had a *fantasma* along."

On inquiry, her cord translated that odd word as *Ghost*. Abbie could have howled in joy. This was confirmation that her instincts were correct in urging her to enter this market. She was on the right trail.

The guard nodded to Emily. "I know you. You're one of Zander's kids. Never seen you alone, before. What are you doing with a Grimm?"

"Bringing her to meet him," Emily said.

The guard's eyebrow rose and his tanned face blanched under his hat. His gaze returned to Abbie with grave apprehension. He gulped, and then he did something extraordinary. He offered the rest of his stones to her. "Go on, take them all."

He dropped the two other stones onto her palm and said, "You'll need them if you plan to tangle with Zander. In a pinch, they might buy you some time."

The new stones were larger than the first and heavier. Their magic also felt powerful. Abbie held them close to her chest, filled with deep gratitude and wonder. Despite her being a Grimm, not only was this guard letting her in, he was helping.

She held his worried gaze a moment, thoughtfully rolling the stones within her fist. Finally, she said the only thing she could. "Thank you."

Handing the small azure stone to Emily, she pocketed the other two next to Ruth in her jacket pocket.

"Once you enter the market, you both must stay together at all times," he warned. "No straying! It's the only way you'll stay alive. The circle will protect you against magical spells."

Extra protection to Arthur's shield. Excellent.

"If that's all, we'll be on our way." Excited to begin their market adventure, Abbie took Emily's hand and hurried toward the circle awaiting them.

As she passed the two guardian statues, her whole body vibrated. Once past the entrance, they both approached the circle, and it expanded to accommodate two. They stepped into it and hovered, like the circle, a few inches above the dirt ground.

The guard who'd followed them grabbed Abbie's wrist. She turned to him in surprise.

He leaned closer, bringing a scent of stale food and fear. "I'm Carlos Ortiz," he whispered, his mustache twitching. "When the battle starts, remember Ortiz helped you."

That sounded ominous. What battle did he mean?

Before she could ask, he released his grip and stepped away, turning to deal with a new arrival.

She set the circle in motion, instructing it to take them to Jimi and Nica. To her utter relief, it instantly moved them deeper into the market. Abbie then asked Hafgufa, *"Check again if you can connect with my kids and our friends."*

"Found the cat shifter," the cord said.

"Yousef," Abbie said, *"I'm in the market."*

"Good," he replied. *"Don't come for me or Vivian."*

"Are you alright?" she asked.

"Can't talk. They're using River to coerce Vivian's cooperation. Don't contact me again or they might notice my movements. Communication is their forte."

"Who are they?"

"I can no longer reach him," Hafgufa said.

That sounded bad. *"How about Robert?"*

"He is weak and unable to respond."

"The children?" Abbie asked, fist clenching as terror soared through her. *"Are they with River, Yousef, or Vivian?"*

"No," Hafgufa said.

Then it might be safe to contact them. *"Try the children."*

"We're here, Abbie!" Nica sounded extremely relieved.

Jimi's excited voice came through next. *"We know where River's being held, but we can't get him out."*

"Are you both safe?" she asked.

"Yes," Nica said. *"We're hiding outside the building where they're holding him."*

"Stay out of sight," she warned them. *"I'm on my way."* Just in case, she mentally asked, *"Arthur, can you sense the kids now?"*

"Yes!"

Brilliant. *"Raise your shield over both of them again."*

He buzzed her in acknowledgment, but warned that his

abilities were now stretched to his limit.

"Noted," Abbie responded.

A prickling at her nape had her glancing back, her attention drawn to one of the griffin statues at the entrance. It had changed shape! It now looked like a gigantic winged female.

Her heart thundered as the statue's uneasy gaze followed her until Abbie turned a corner and lost sight of her.

Like the wish stones had reminded Abbie of her wish bombs, that griffin-turned-winged woman was also familiar. The giantess with wings was strikingly reminiscent of the angel on the stained-glass panel at St. Michael's.

Chapter Ten

They whizzed past patrons who had stopped their circles to inspect wares at stalls, with Abbie keeping her eyes open for any danger signs. "Emily."

"Yes?" the little girl asked.

"What did those two giant statues look like to you at the entrance to the market?"

"Like two beasts with wings," Emily said.

"Did one of them change shape at any point?"

Emily's gaze grew worried as she stared at Abbie. "No. Did one change shape for you?"

"Yes," Abbie said, bemused. Could this be a sign her prayer was about to be answered? That suggested anyone could pray and receive a response. One just had to believe it was possible. Did Nica simply have that belief down in spades? "Have you ever met an angel?"

Emily shook her head. "I think my mummy once told me an angel would watch over me. But Zander said mine left after my mummy died because the angel didn't like me."

At those heartbreaking words, Abbie's Grimm instinct shouted she'd reached a crossroads with this child. Instinctively, she said, "Stop!"

Their transport circle halted in place. Abbie was stunned by the circle's instant response. Feeling more confident about her control of the circle, she told it to continue to their destination.

When it did so, trusting the circle to carry them to Jimi and Nica without her monitoring it every minute, Abbie knelt to speak to the girl eye-to-eye. "Emily, I, too, used to think angels weren't real until I saw one just now."

"Ooh," Emily said, wide-eyed with wonder.

"I'm sure of one thing, though," Abbie continued.

"What's that?"

"Your angel would have loved you because you are very loveable. Do you know how I know that?"

Emily shook her head, her hand tightening its grip on Abbie's fingers.

"Because I loved you the first moment we met," she said.

Emily gasped and then reached for a hug. Her arms wrapped around Abbie's neck as she broke into sobs.

Abbie held her like that, letting her cry out her hurts, dashed dreams, and hopes, gently stroking her back. Such a tiny, vulnerable thing to undergo so much pain and abuse.

As the child's sobs grew quieter, Abbie said, "Emily."

"Yes?" she replied in a whisper and hiccupped.

"I want you to question some things that Zander has told you. I suspect he might have lied. Okay?"

The child leaned back. "Why? Why would he lie?"

Abbie unearthed a clean tissue from a back pocket and gave it to Emily to wipe her face and blow her nose. "He doesn't have your compulsion talent and so, he might have decided the best way to get you to do what he wants is to fib."

"Do you fib to get people to do things?" Emily asked.

Abbie nodded. "Sometimes. Most everyone does."

The child frowned, the now-soiled tissue scrunched up in her fist. "How can I know when someone's fibbing?"

"The way I tell is to place my hand over my heart, close my eyes, and ask myself, is what I'm hearing true? Then, if I'm quiet, and listen, keeping my heart and mind open to hearing the truth, even if it's difficult to hear, deep inside me, I'll know if the person speaks the truth. Want to try?"

Emily nodded frantically.

Abbie took Emily's hand and placed it over the child's heart and then said, "Now ask me a question. I'll answer, and you tell me if what I've told you is the truth."

Emily shut her eyes. "Do you love Jimi and Nica?"

"Yes."

"True. Do you want to find them?"

"No. I don't care if I find them or not."

Emily's eyes snapped open wide. "You're lying!" Then she shut her eyes again. "Will you take me to Zander like you said you would?"

"Yes," Abbie replied, "but I won't leave you with him."

Emily frowned and opened her eyes. "Why not?"

"Because I want you to be safe at home with your mummy."

"But she's dead."

"That is what Zander said to you." Abbie put her hand to her own heart. "But in here, I don't believe him."

Emily's mouth hung open as she stared at Abbie.

As the child thought about that, Abbie smelled an enticing scent from a food vendor they passed. Guilt at depriving Emily of those crisps at the mall had her asking the circle to stop.

"Emily, are you hungry?" Abbie asked.

The girl nodded, still frowning. "Yes."

Abbie asked their circle to return to the food vendor. The circle soon halted before a stall staffed by a tall woman wearing a pretty dress and a headscarf.

"How may I help you two?" the vendor asked.

"Show her your stone," Abbie said to Emily. Once the girl placed the blue stone on the counter, Abbie asked, "What can we purchase to eat for that?"

The woman glanced at the stone, and then at the two of them over her counter. Giving a nod, she turned to fetch two large pasties, wrapped them in paper, and handed one to each. Then she pushed the blue stone back toward Emily. "You can keep this for when you get hungry next."

"How do we pay for these, then?" Abbie asked, hesitant to bite the warm pasty despite her mouth watering in longing.

"A Grimm and her guest get to eat for free at my stall," the food vendor replied.

How had this stall owner known Abbie was a Grimm? She glanced warily at her food and then at Emily, wondering if she should warn her about eating it, but the child was already well into her meal.

Sighing in resignation, Abbie took a bite, chewed, and swallowed. "It's delicious."

"Good," the vendor said and smiled widely, revealing a missing tooth. "My name is Jakka Blake. When the fighting begins, remember that Jakka helped you."

Abbie glanced at the stall owner with worry. "Both you and the entry guard have mentioned a fight. Why?"

The woman raised an eyebrow, as if surprised by the query. "It's foretold, mistress. Once a Grimm enters the Spell Gate, the time of battle will begin."

"Between whom?" Abbie asked.

The woman shrugged. "Only you know that. It's why the market forbids Grimms here. Why they changed the transport circles to defend the customers they move about. No one would dare attack a person while they were within one, without risking the attack reflecting on them."

She indicated her stall. "Shopkeepers are not so lucky. We have to fend for ourselves. So, I'm going to close up for the day. I have a family waiting for my return. Safe travels."

She pulled down the shutter, and a click sounded as it locked. Then a shield shimmered around the stall, forcing the circle to retreat.

Curious. Abbie had no intention of starting a fight. Still, she was glad to be within the circle and asked it to continue toward Jimi and Nica's location.

Emily, having finished eating her pasty in record time, glanced up at Abbie's barely touched one with interest. Crumbs covered the girl's mouth. Abbie contemplated sharing half of hers and risk Emily having a tummy ache from eating too much. A disturbance ahead drew her focus.

"Stop," Abbie said.

Their circle halted in a crowded plaza this time. Directly ahead, people backed away as someone advanced.

Abbie shifted Emily behind her and gave her the rest of her pasty. "Stay out of sight, but within this circle."

A female, clothed in a long, colorful, flowing scarf that circled her sensually, strode toward Abbie with purpose.

Alarmed cries rang out as people scurried out of the way, leaving a barren space between Abbie and the newcomer. The approaching woman had features that were remarkably similar to Kiros Hillier, the Earth companion. Only her skin color leaned toward greenish rather than inky.

"Who is that?" Emily whispered in a fearful tone, clutching Abbie's pasty and peering around her jean-clad leg.

"I think this might be Tuuli," Abbie whispered. No longer a light ethereal being by the gate, this time she presented herself as a fearsome woman twice Abbie's height. "She's the market's security agent."

"Oh, Zander told me about her," Emily said, sliding out of sight behind Abbie.

Abbie twisted to glance at the child. "What did he say?"

"That he would have to give me up to her if I misbehaved. He said she's a she-devil. That she killed his parents when he was little, just as she killed mine." Emily paused and then asked, "Did he fib about that, Abbie? I felt sorry that she'd killed his parents. If my mummy's alive, could his parents be alive, too?"

"I don't know," Abbie said and faced the woman, who was now less than five meters ahead.

"Zander would be happy to learn his parents were alive," Emily murmured. "I'd like to make him happy."

Abbie spared a bothered backward glance. Even as she took one step forward by convincing Emily to see Zander as a liar, the child stepped back by wanting to please her abuser.

However, her immediate concern was Tuuli. The woman carried no weapons, but in this magical place, that meant little. If not for Arthur and her circle that protected against magical attacks, Tuuli could probably twitch her nose and blow a hole straight through Abbie.

She mentally alerted her cord to be ready.

Hafgufa slid out of Abbie's right forefinger, circling below her hand in a spark-spitting golden energy tether.

Tuuli stopped her advance, her gaze narrowing on the cord.

Hafgufa had a reputation for having killed a god. Vivian confirmed that when she said her water goddess had once killed a fire god. Abbie suspected the other gods may have imprisoned Hafgufa as a cord in punishment.

Abbie's spirit now reared, straightening her spine. If the only way she could save her children and Emily was by killing this companion, so be it.

"No," Hafgufa said.

"What?" Abbie asked, surprised by the cord's response. It rarely spoke without being spoken to.

"I can communicate," Hafgufa said, *"compel people to release information, and confine, but I am forbidden to kill."*

A glance at Emily, who was looking around the gathering crowd, suggested that Hafgufa wasn't sharing this news with the child.

"If I do," the cord added, *"I will die. You'll end up with an ordinary cord dropped by your feet, no longer a formidable weapon within your arm. Those are the terms of my confinement."*

Abbie drew in a sharp breath at the diminishing choices at her disposal. Arthur had reached his limits and Hafgufa was no longer a killer. Good to know one's restrictions.

A movement to her immediate left startled Abbie. She glanced that way, but everyone had retreated far from her and Tuuli. Yet, she could have sworn she'd seen someone nearby.

"Emily." Abbie pointed with her thumb. "Do you see anyone over there?"

"No," the child said.

"I am here," a soft voice murmured.

No one was physically there, not that Abbie could see. She was about to shift her sight, the way her mother had taught her to see a person's aura, when Emily spoke.

"Abbie, Zander is in the crowd." Emily aimed her finger to

the left. "He wants me to come."

Abbie's left hand whipped behind her and latched onto Emily's arm. Her pulse pounded in terror that she was in imminent danger of losing track of this abused child.

"Don't leave me," she said, her words perfectly calm, though she didn't know how she kept her dread out. "Stay a while and we'll go find him later, alright?"

"Okay," Emily said, though Abbie couldn't tell without looking if the child was reluctant or glad. For now, Abbie's instinct warned her to keep Emily out of Tuuli's line of sight, so she kept her behind her back.

From the corner of her eye, Abbie again sensed someone nearby, just out of sight. No solid visual cues, but waves of positive energy buffeted her on that side.

She was careful not to look directly at her unknown company. That helped Abbie better see her visitor's shadow. A tall woman with wings. Though she knew who it had to be, she gulped and asked, "Are you my stained-glass angel?"

"Yes," the angel said, not aloud, but inside Abbie's mind. She sounded surprised, and a little bemused by the question. *"You sensed my presence as a child?"*

"Yes. Why did you never speak to me?" Abbie asked.

"Not our place to interfere with our charge's free will."

"Not even when we need you?" Abbie asked, brought down to earth by that dispassionate response.

"In each moment of your life, what you perceive is simply a spark of what is happening. We view that same moment along a kaleidoscope of your life's intended path. While you might believe you are in dire need, we might view that same event as exactly what must happen for your greater good."

Slowly, the angel's celestial view of life penetrated Abbie's consciousness. She was stunned by the sheer unemotional, analytical viewpoint. If angels were real, she'd assumed they would be loving, sweet, and caring.

Humans rarely saw or spoke to these celestial watchdogs and were likely unaware of an angel's true role. Films like *The Bishop's Wife* and religious institutions cemented that error by painting angels as benevolent and helpful. They might be both those things, but a vaulted viewpoint skewed their interactions with those they safeguarded.

This raised another question.

"Why show yourself now?" Abbie asked.

"Market authorities foretold and countered your arrival, Guardian," the angel said in a detached tone. *"Our interference is required to rebalance likely outcomes."*

"For the greater good?" Abbie asked.

The angel nodded.

Then a word the angel used registered. She'd called Abbie, *Guardian*. Too many other supernatural creatures had inexplicably addressed her that way, too, including Kiros. Abbie could no longer discount that was her role in this life.

Unlike her mother and grandmother, who had both been Grimms, Abbie was a *Grimm Guardian*, at whose touch all their artifacts had come alive.

Now an angel helped her? She didn't know if she should be thrilled or terrified. What was she about to face that needed an angelic assist? Could it have something to do with this upcoming fight she'd been hearing about?

The shadow extended her arm and pointed at Abbie's circle. Her transport unit instantly glowed blindingly white, like a halo on the ground.

Nearby patrons gasped and pointed her way.

Soon the circle faded to its paler form.

"Must have been a malfunction," Abbie said aloud.

That seemed to calm those around them, as the words "faulty" and "defective" were passed around.

Abbie turned to the angel and whispered, "What have you done to my Uber circle?"

"I've severed its connection to the market, putting it under your full control. Use that ability wisely."

It wasn't the help she would have asked for. She could have used wings to fly to take her past Tuuli or a map that showed where her kids and friends were. "The entrance guard said the circle was already under my control."

"Yes, while you remained in the market confines. To do what you must, you will need to travel outside those restrictive boundaries." The angel's shadow arm pointed toward Tuuli. *"This is a distraction. Go finish your mission. Hurry!"*

"Why, what's happened?" Abbie asked.

But her invisible visitor was gone. The angel had left without saying where Abbie should hurry off to. She'd have to stick to her original plan to find her kids and hope it wasn't Vivian or Yousef who was in dire trouble and needed immediate help.

"Who are you talking to?" Emily asked, confused.

"An angel," Abbie said absently. Before she could elaborate, Tuuli spoke, drawing her attention.

"You will leave this market now!"

"Can't just yet," Abbie replied in a pleasant tone. "I'm here to find my children. Have you seen them? They go by Nica and

Jimi. If you help me locate them, we'll all be out of your green hair in no time."

The woman's head tilted as she flicked her luscious green locks back to study Abbie with an insolent smile. "If they're here, they are no longer your concern." She gave a careless shrug. "The market will decide their fates."

Abbie's hands fisted at that pitiless declaration. "They matter to me. Since you're unwilling to help, I'll be on my way."

"Show you have a modicum of sense," Tuuli snapped, "and leave this market of your own volition. Or I will assist you and, believe me, Grimm, you won't enjoy that experience."

Abbie's temper flared at that overt threat. She'd met a musical fae queen once. That monarch was more talk than substance, literally. The fae had presented herself as huge when, in actuality, she could have fit within Abbie's palm. The fae queen also showed little respect for other life forms, even those she ruled. She had transformed one of her subjects into a pair of her sandals.

At that memory, Tuuli's lively dress drew Abbie's gaze. How her gown moved was almost as if it had a will of its own. A mischievous thought crossed Abbie's mind.

"That's a pretty gown," she said. "Is it alive?"

The smug smile on Tuuli's face was replaced by a hard glare. Had Abbie hit the nail on the head with her question?

Surely not? But if so, what a very cruel way to treat her servants. Making them inanimate objects to serve her whim. It did, however, match Tuuli's cavalier attitude about Abbie's missing kids.

"Maybe that creature would prefer to do something other than clothe you?" Abbie mused aloud. "Shall we ask?"

If that gown was truly a living creature, Abbie didn't have the authority to override Tuuli's command. Did Tuuli know that, though? There seemed to be lots of false rumors flying around about a Grimm's abilities.

Her brothers often insisted that sometimes faking self-assurance could be as effective as true confidence.

Unhappy with looking up at Tuuli, Abbie asked the circle to rise until she faced Tuuli head-on. Satisfied with the leveling of at least one factor in this confrontation, Abbie spoke with the full force of her Grimm heritage shoring up her backbone. "No one should control another."

She was also, in part, speaking to Emily.

Behind her, the child gasped.

Her words, having affected at least one of her audiences, boosted Abbie's courage and she pointed dramatically to Tuuli's gown. "Gown, you are free to go."

Tuuli's glance flew from Abbie's finger to her gown with obvious alarm.

Abbie whispered to her circle to take her and Emily to her kids at top speed. Now!

They instantly whizzed around Tuuli, traveling so fast, Abbie had to struggle to stay upright. As their departure sped up with each passing moment, she turned and clutched Emily to her to steady the child.

In the distance, a scream of fury rose, reverberating like a siren of alarm. Had her fake-out worked, or was Tuuli upset Abbie had fled before she could throw her out of the market? Likely the latter.

Chapter Eleven

By the time her circle stopped, the air had grown blessedly quiet. Abbie found herself beside a building that looked remarkably like the recital hall in Kent. Yet, a glance up showed no sun in sight, even though the day was still bright. That meant they were still inside the market.

"Psst," someone said from nearby.

Abbie glanced in that direction and saw a small hand gesture for her to come toward a row of bushes. She was about to step over there and then remembered she wasn't supposed to leave the circle.

"Over there," she said, and the circle moved her and Emily toward the hand. Jimi and Nica were crouched behind a large bush. Abbie's relief overwhelmed her and brought her to her knees.

She opened her arms and her kids' circle brought them closer, but it couldn't enter Abbie's circle. She instructed her circle to allow Nica and Jimi inside and, as soon as they crossed over, the two kids hugged her tight.

"It's not supposed to do that," Emily said, frowning at the smaller circle now fully within the larger one. "Only a guard can allow a circle to expand to include people. And circles don't go into other circles. At least, I've never seen one do that."

"Ours must be special then," Abbie said. That angel must have indeed altered her circle to respond to all of Abbie's wishes. She sent a silent *Thank you* to her, but didn't hear a response.

"Are you both alright?" Abbie asked, cherishing holding

her children safely in her arms.

"We're okay," Nica said, hugging her close.

Jimi nodded his head.

"Where's Robert?" Abbie asked next, and held her breath, afraid her kids were about to tell her he had vanished permanently. Is that why he wasn't with them? He would never willingly leave them unguarded.

Nica pointed to the hall. "He's watching River in there. Abbie, he can't move from place to place as he used to. Here, he can only go into a room if someone opens a door. And..."

"Yes?" Abbie asked, relieved that at least he was still around, even if weakened.

"I don't think he's well," Nica whispered. "I can barely see him anymore and once he faded away altogether before reappearing. We haven't seen him now for hours."

"He told us River is in trouble," Jimi added, "and that he was using all his strength to hide him. The way Robert hid us from the demon in St. Michael's church." Jimi then added, "He asked us to wait out here for help. That Yousef and Vivian would come, but they didn't. I'm so glad you did."

Nica looked torn. "I wanted to check on Robert, Abbie, but I promised not to let go of Jimi's hand, so I didn't. Not once."

"Good girl!" She kissed Nica's cheek. "Well done on keeping your brother safe. But both of you were wrong to get into that stranger's car. You understand that, right?"

Nica nodded. "I tried calling Kali, but she didn't answer. Is she angry with me, too?"

"I'm not angry," Abbie said. "I'm disappointed in both of your behaviors and there will be consequences once we return home."

"Like what?" Jimi asked.

Abbie tilted her head to study the young lad. She normally gave him lots of leeway. Had it been too much? "No jam for you for a month," she said. Jam was his favorite food. He asked for it at breakfast every morning.

Jimi's jaw dropped, and then his mouth formed a pout.

"As for you, young lady," Abbie said, turning to Nica.

"I'll give up jam, too," she said in a hurry.

Abbie shook her head. "You'll give up cleaning for a month."

Nica's face now dropped in horror. The OCD child in her must be in shock at the suggestion.

"As for Kali, I don't think she's angry with you, either," Abbie said. "There seem to be lots of rules and barriers to the use of magic in here."

Emily, who had been following this exchange, stepped forward and said, "Abbie's rules are less painful than Zander's."

Nica's gaze turned critical as she pointed to her. "Why is she here?"

"This is Emily," Abbie said, drawing the girl forward. "She helped me get into the market."

"Zander is looking for you," Jimi said, helpfully.

"How do you know that?" Abbie asked.

"The fake hall told me," he said.

Of course it did.

Nica let go of her brother long enough to use both her hands to separate Abbie's hold on Emily. Then she took Abbie and Jimi's hands in hers, pulling her brother beside her. "She's mine. And so is Jimi. You can't have either of them. If you try,

I'll set a goddess on you and you won't like that."

"Nica," Abbie said in warning as tears budded in Emily's eyes. "That wasn't nice."

"Jimi says she's bad," Nica said in a firm tone. "She's the one who has been talking kids into leaving their homes to come to this market and that awful hall."

Emily cried now, covering her face.

Jimi looked as if he were about to cry, too.

Abbie released her hold on Nica to bring a distressed Emily into her hold. Then she faced her two children. "Okay, I understand the situation. This is good to know. However, Zander took Emily from her family, too, lied to her, and hurt her for years. Can you imagine what that must have felt like?"

Jimi nodded.

Nica's lips pressed in a tight line and she stubbornly raised her chin.

Abbie gently brushed a finger across her beautiful daughter's face. This child was usually the one who was most compassionate and loving. For her to be this reticent, she must have been terrified after losing track of Abbie. Poor little angel.

"Nica," Abbie said in a gentle voice, pulling Nica close, "weren't you frightened last night after you and I became separated? When that car took you and Jimi away?"

The little girl's chin wobbled, and she nodded her head. Eyes tearing, she dropped her gaze to the ground.

"That's how Emily must have felt when someone took her from her mother," Abbie continued. "After years with her captors, she's forgotten what it was like to have people around who love her and care about her. She's been told she can't eat anything but porridge and, if she does anything that Zander disapproves of, she's not allowed to eat for two days."

"Nothing?" Nica asked, gaze rising to look at Emily with shock and worry.

Now there was her little girl. It thrilled Abbie to see the caring look return to Nica's face.

"That's Zander's rule number four," Emily said in a subdued voice and met Abbie's gaze. "Was that wrong?"

"Yes, Emily, he made up that rule and he shouldn't have done it."

"Are all his rules fibs?"

Abbie nodded, and Emily shivered.

"I can now make six tasty dishes," Nica told Emily. "Granny Chan's been teaching us. If you like, I'll make you one of them when we get home."

Abbie's heart went out to her generous child.

"And I'll help," Jimi offered. "After we rescue River."

"Even though you both hate me?" Emily asked in wonder.

"If you promise to stop hurting other kids," Nica said, drawing her line in this sandbox, "then we can be friends."

"What's that?" Emily asked, frowning in confusion.

"When you are friends with other kids," Jimi explained, "you get to pinkie swear and do fun things like that. River is mine. We came here to find him 'cause he's in trouble. Friends watch out for each other."

"But what is a friend?" Emily asked.

Abbie stayed silent, letting these three work this out for themselves, while her gaze flicked across the street as she gauged how to get into the hall.

"Friends are kids who are nice to each other," Jimi explained in all seriousness, sounding wise beyond his years.

"I have lots of them and Jimi has one," Nica said. "I'll introduce you to mine."

"Oh, I'd like one, too," Emily said. "I don't have any."

Abbie, half-listening to this heartwarming conversation, realized Nica was right. Her little girl had lots of friends, while Jimi had only formed one close friendship. No wonder he was so determined to come to River's rescue.

As for Emily, admitting no one had been nice to her was simply heartbreaking.

"I can help you find River," Emily said, stepping away from Abbie, as if she wanted to earn the right to be Nica and Jimi's friend.

"We know where he is," Jimi said, pointing to the hall across the street. "He's in there with Robert. We don't know how to get him out."

"I know how," Emily said.

"How can you help?" Jimi asked Emily, sounding as suspicious now as his sister had been earlier.

"I'm good at convincing people to do what I want."

"Will that help, Abbie?" the boy asked, uncertain.

"It could." Abbie pulled Jimi closer, and he leaned into her hold, showing how worried he was for River. Rightfully so. If Robert was as weak as Nica intimated, they might lose both him and River if they didn't act quickly. "We won't leave the market without River and Robert."

Jimi whispered, "Thank you."

She caught Nica's worried gaze. "And Robert will be fine once we're home."

Nica joined in the hug and then, after hesitating a moment, Emily did, too, tentatively, as if she were unused to such loving gestures. Emily gave Nica Abbie's pasty that she hadn't finished.

"Thanks," Nica said, and broke it in half to share with Jimi.

Satisfied, Abbie told everyone to link hands. "We need to plan our next move, but lingering here is unsafe." She'd probably stayed too long already. That angel's, *Hurry!* rang in her ears.

"Hang on," she said and ordered her circle to move in random directions anywhere it wished while she and the kids decided on their next steps. That should temporarily keep anyone tracking her or the kids off their trail.

The circle immediately took them to haphazard locations. It was difficult to focus on plans when they passed through the most amazing neighborhoods. From bizarre cloud communities to what looked like celestial realms. There was even one entirely underwater. As Klaus had shown, the Spell Gate realm had compounds to house various types of life forms. Those were situated outside the immediate market environs where vendors operated shops.

Could this ability to visit these extraordinary locations be the result of the change the angel had enacted on her circle? Likely. She doubted market customers normally visited other creatures' encampments that were inhospitable to them.

"If this fake hall is the same as the one in Kent," Abbie said, forcing herself to concentrate. "River and Robert are likely in the hidden room. If we use the main or back doors to enter the hall, even with Ruth hiding us, the iron in the hidden doorway will strip all magic on entry and they'll spot us."

"We could use the tunnel," Emily said.

"Good idea," Abbie replied. "If there's one here."

"There is," Emily said. "I've been in it."

"Good," Abbie said, "then that's our best way inside."

She asked the circle to take them to a safe opening that would lead into the tunnel.

Instead of carrying them to the street where Abbie and Seamus had exited the tunnel, the circle took them into the woods. This section was darker than the other sections they'd visited. Here, moving shadows and spots of lights flitted about. She guessed this might be the fae encampment. Abbie expected to turn around and meet Tuuli.

The circle stopped.

Straight ahead was a giant tree. Looked like a yew, bigger than any she'd ever seen. This specimen had a beautiful reddish-brown trunk with flat green needles and gigantic branches. Oddly, she gained the impression this tree watched them. Two of its branches were folded across each other, and it displayed what appeared to be a frown at the very top.

"This isn't the human zone," the tree said, speaking in a slow, deep, lumbering tone. *"You shouldn't be able to be here. You'll be in serious trouble if security finds out."*

"We'd appreciate it if you didn't tell security," Abbie replied, swallowing her surprise at speaking to a tree. Could it hear her way up there? Did it have ears? "We're trying to rescue a child and a ghost," she said, raising her voice. "We need to use a tunnel that is around here somewhere."

Even as she spoke, a quick scan confirmed nothing resembling an opening on the ground nearby. Why had her circle brought them here then?

"Oh, ho, I know you," the giant yew said to Abbie, pointing a branch. "You're the Grimm that everyone's talking about. You disrobed Queen Tuuli in the market."

"I did?" Abbie asked. She'd hoped to distract Tuuli, maybe have her fight to control the cloth. Not humiliate her.

"Her gown flew away after you said no one may control another."

Abbie cringed, picturing herself being shamed in front of all those she oversaw. Tuuli would never forgive her for such an affront. That also explained the scream reigning over the market as she and Emily fled, and why Tuuli hadn't come for her yet. She'd thoroughly distracted her. But when Tuuli tracked Abbie down, she could imagine her fury.

"I'm sorry about that. I will tell her so the next time we meet." Abbie shifted the kids behind her, in case this fae creature decided it should avenge its queen's disgrace. "I didn't mean to upset her."

The tree chuckled, which sounded like branches cracking. She'd amused the yew instead of offending it. Did that mean the fae were not so fond of Tuuli? Interesting.

Abbie couldn't resist asking the tree, "Why do you put up with Tuuli's high-handedness?"

"If we don't, we'd end up as her gown or hat." The tree shrugged. "After they placed her in charge of the market, her powerful siblings said she could call on her kin during emergencies. Ever since then, no one's dared question her orders. Until you arrived." He seemed to focus on her circle. "How did you do that? Circles can't leave the market grounds, and this compound is outside the market."

Before she could come up with a plausible answer, he glanced to the right. "You better get going. The queen's on her way here and not too happy with you. I'll give you a head start and point her in the wrong direction."

"You would do that for us?" Abbie asked, surprised and relieved.

The tree nodded.

"Why are you helping us?" Abbie asked, curious.

He smiled wide, revealing a deep tree hollow. "My name is Oliver. When the fighting starts, remember that Oliver helped you, Grimm. Now go."

"Thank you," she said, no longer questioning that familiar refrain to remember who helped her.

The kids added their thanks.

"Time to enter the tunnel," Abbie said to her circle. Since she couldn't find the trapdoor, maybe the circle could. At her words, the ground beneath their feet dropped away.

Abbie's circle fell, taking them with it. The kids screamed. Or was Abbie doing that? She gasped, out of breath and terrified. They finally came to a smooth halt, but by then, her throat felt sore and swollen. Straight ahead was a familiar tunnel.

"Everyone all right?" Abbie asked, releasing the children she'd been clutching during their precipitous plunge.

All three kids nodded.

"That was so cool." Jimi sounded more excited than frightened.

"It was worse than riding Comet," Nica said, unimpressed.

"Who's Comet?" Emily asked.

"A witch's broom," Nica explained.

"Let's crack on," Abbie said. "Robert and River are counting on us, and Oliver might not buy us a lot of time to get this done. Circle, take us to the recital hall's hidden room."

The circle whizzed them down a tunnel that was tall enough that Abbie didn't have to scrunch down as they sped along its twisty curvy path. Once the circle stopped, they were at a dead end. On the wall straight ahead, a metal ladder led upward. At the ceiling, three meters up, she spotted a closed trapdoor lighted by a lit sconce.

"That light being on means a watcher is in the cage room upstairs," Emily whispered. "When someone turns on the lights upstairs, this one comes on, too."

Abbie nodded. "Good to know. I'll wait for the light to go out before heading up there."

"I want to come, too," Jimi said.

Abbie knelt and brought him around to make eye contact. She spoke clearly so he would understand her clearly. "Jimi, I need you to stay here and guard our way out of here once we have rescued River and Robert. We won't be able to escape if someone is here on my return. Your job is to speak to this tunnel so it can warn you if there's a threat approaching down that passageway. Will you do that?"

"Yes," he said, sounding reluctant, but resigned.

Nica took his hand. "I'll stay with him, Abbie."

"Good girl," Abbie said.

"I have to come with you," Emily said, "or you won't be able to get River to leave."

"Why not?" Abbie asked.

Emily hung her head.

Abbie tilted Emily's face up by her chin. At seeing the tremendous remorse reflected in her gaze, she took the child's left hand and placed it over Emily's heart. "Do you remember how you tell when someone speaks the truth?"

Emily nodded, tears budding in her eyes.

"Good, then listen to what I'm about to say and see if you can feel in your heart if I'm telling the truth. All right?"

Emily frowned, but agreed.

"Whatever you tell me," Abbie said. "I won't be upset. I will believe that you did the best you could."

Emily's tightly pressed lips trembled.

Nica came over and put her arm around the little girl's shoulders. "Us, too."

Jimi frowned at Emily and then at his sister. Finally, he nodded and put his arm around Emily's waist. "It's okay. We won't hate you. I promise."

"Are we telling the truth, Emily?" Abbie asked.

The child nodded, tears streaming down her face.

"Then tell us. Why won't I be able to get River out?"

"Zander had me tell him to stay put in his cage," Emily whispered, her voice choked. "He makes me do that with all the kids until he's ready to send them to their new homes. I'm so sorry."

Abbie hugged all three children. "That's all right. All that matters is that you want to help River now."

She finally understood how and why this horrid Zander had used Emily to imprison other children. No wonder he took her with him everywhere. Why he wanted her back. Her "compelling" talent made her his most valuable tool.

Nica stepped back, her eyes wide open with equal understanding. "That's why Robert couldn't convince River to leave the hidden room, isn't it? Why he had to stay with River. He can't leave his cage."

Abbie nodded, her hope rising at this shocking news. "If so, with Emily's help, it should be possible to get both Robert and River out."

Jimi released his hold on Emily and patted her shoulder. "Thank you for helping us save River now."

Her generous-hearted kids left Abbie supremely proud. She pulled out Ruth, her magical mirror. "I was going to do this for me, but if Emily is coming along, we can ensure she isn't seen either."

About to tap Ruth, Abbie paused, a shudder running through her as the peril she was about to take Emily into, to rescue another child, sank in.

Nica laid a hand on Abbie's arm as if she sensed her trepidation. "You always say we mustn't let fear control what we do. I'm scared, but I won't let that stop me from saving River and Robert."

"Me, either," Jimi said.

"Or me," Emily said with a firm nod. "Never again."

Her words left Abbie choked up with joy. The frightened little girl cowering under a bush that Abbie and Seamus encountered last night had come a long way.

"Thank you," she said. "All of you. Now let's show fear who's boss."

Chapter Twelve

"If someone comes down this tunnel," Abbie said to her kids, "before Emily and I return from up in the cage room, it would be better if no one sees you both. So, let's get Ruth to make us all invisible. Ready?"

All three kids nodded.

Abbie tapped her mirror once to signal Ruth to make everyone invisible.

"I can still see you," Emily said.

Abbie took out Ruth and showed Emily that they were all invisible except to each other.

"Wow," Emily said, "it even made your circle invisible, Abbie."

When she glanced in the mirror, only the kids' smaller circle was visible.

Odd. Unless this was a reaction to Abbie's circle now belonging entirely to her, while the kids' circle remained connected to the market. That might be why it hadn't vanished when they were in the fae compound, which was outside the market. Because it had been within Abbie's circle.

Then another fascinating thought occurred. Did the fact Ruth had made Abbie's circle invisible mean her circle had awoken like all her other artifacts? Was that why her instruction to Ruth to turn "everyone" invisible had included her circle, but not Jimi and Nica's circle, which was still an inanimate object?

One way to find out.

"Jimi, ask my circle if it's real. A living thing."

He gave her a startled look and then focused on her circle. "Are you alive?" Jimi listened for a moment and then faced her. "He says yes, and his name is Eli."

Abbie allowed that incredible news to sink in. In severing her circle's connection to the market, had the angel gifted her with an artifact? And because she was the Grimm Guardian, had Eli now awoken?

An incredible sense of gratitude overwhelmed her. Was this how her ancestors felt whenever they received a magical artifact? Would she be able to take Eli back to Kent?

What a magnificent gift for a magic-less Grimm that was likely to face danger every day of her life!

Just then, the light switched off above them, bathing them in darkness.

"It's time," Abbie said, but she didn't care to leave while the kids' circle remained visible. "Ruth, turn the children's circle invisible, too, please."

Her mirror complied.

"All right then, Emily, let's go free Robert and River," she said with renewed confidence. She kissed Nica and Jimi and told them to stay safe.

If Jimi heard of anyone coming down the tunnel, they were to come to her. She couldn't send them to Oliver, since their circle couldn't pass beyond the market's boundaries.

Once the two circles separated, Abbie had Eli raise Emily and her upward, toward the trapdoor.

At the top, Emily's hand reached for the light switch. Abbie caught her hand to stop her from turning it on. She didn't want to tip off anyone to their presence. Who knew if these villains had installed a CCTV camera or a magical scrying one to monitor the room above?

She slowly raised the trapdoor and listened. All was quiet in the upper cage room. Once the circle took them up to the floor above, she silently laid the trapdoor flat.

It was dark in here, with no windows to let in moonlight or sunlight. A dim sliver of light flashed from the far corner of the room, eerily flicking on and off.

"That light never turns off completely," Emily whispered, and took Abbie's hand. The circle took them further into the room, following Emily's lead, toward a cage at the other end. This must hold River, where Robert now hid him from sight.

It was like moving blindfolded, but Abbie trusted Emily knew where to direct Eli.

"Here," the child whispered, laying Abbie's hand over the lock on the door.

Abbie had Hafgufa come out of her forefinger and insert into the lock. The cord shaped itself into a key and unlocked the door. When that distinctive click sounded, Abbie gently pulled the door open. It creaked a little.

Kneeling by the opening, she said, "It's Abbie. Anyone I know in here?"

"Miss Grimshaw?" he asked in a shaky, surprised voice in her head. *"You came for us! I told River you would find a way."*

Those were the sweetest words Abbie had ever heard. She would remember them for the rest of her life. Robert had trusted her to save not only himself but River.

"River?" Abbie called.

"I'm here," the boy said, sounding suspicious. "But where are you? Is this another trick?"

Abbie tapped her jacket pocket twice to signal Ruth to end

the hide-me spell. She mentally added to only end it over her and Emily.

"Oh," River said, and then scrambled toward them but stopped at the doorway.

"Emily, tell him he can come out," Abbie said.

"Hi, River," Emily said, moving closer.

Abbie heard the magical vibration in her voice and pictured her small hand covering her throat.

"It's safe for you to come out now," the girl said.

The boy crawled out and straight into Abbie's arms.

She held his shaking little body tight, rocking him and repeatedly telling him he was safe.

Finally, he leaned back and whispered a heartfelt, "Thank you!"

"You're welcome," Abbie said. "Your parents sent me. They were anxious about you and are eager to get you home."

Robert crawled out next, and Emily helped him stand.

Abbie spotted the shadow of the little girl holding up the tall man. He gripped his cane with a shaky hand and rested the other on Emily's slender shoulders.

He was probably fighting to not lean heavily on her. Ever the gentleman, her Robert.

"Time to go," she said, getting to her feet.

"It is indeed," a male voice said, and bright lights came on, blinding Abbie.

Someone slow clapped. "Congratulations, Miss Grimshaw. I've been trying to find that child all day, and you uncovered him in less than a few seconds. Your Grimm reputation is well earned."

Abbie clutched River's hand and shifted herself so she

stood in front of River and Emily. Was this Zander? Must be. She alerted Hafgufa and sent the cord down the back of her jean-clad leg. The cord then slithered along the ground in a slender thread of gold that followed the cracks in the concrete floor. It headed toward the intruder standing outside Eli. Once it reached him, it rose to wrap, ever so gently, around his left ankle.

"And you're traveling without your assigned circle," the man mused. "That is very brave or extremely foolish. Either way, it works to my advantage. Release the boy," he said. "And Emily, come out from behind the lady. Now!"

The last word came out like a whip striking its target.

Abbie squeezed Emily's hand, holding her in place to prevent the girl from coming into the open. The child was shaking in Abbie's hold, as was River.

Abbie, however, felt steady as a rock.

Robert limped closer. *"I do not have the strength left to shield anyone,"* he said, his words sliding into her mind.

A side glance and a few clarifying blinks confirmed he could barely keep himself visible. Zander hadn't mentioned a ghost, which meant he couldn't see Robert. Good.

"Check on Jimi and Nica," she replied in mind-speak. *"They're in the tunnel. I've got this."*

She suggested that mostly to get him out of there safely and to keep Jimi from coming up to rescue River or her. That boy was both brave and incredibly impulsive.

Robert's stubborn glance met hers. He must realize in his current state he couldn't be of much help, yet he was prepared to spend his last moments keeping her safe. Her heart warmed at his protective instincts, but she couldn't allow him to make such a sacrifice.

"I have Hafgufa and Arthur," she reminded him and then added an extra enticement to quit this battlefield. *"The children have no one but you."*

The fight left him. With a nod, he limped away before he vanished down the trapdoor. Knowing he was safe and that the children wouldn't be alone made Abbie feel infinitely better. The fate of River cowering behind her was still uncertain. It was up to her to finish what Robert had begun in safeguarding this boy.

The man confronting Abbie held out his hand to Emily. He was tall, balding, with a lean face and narrow eyes.

"Come here, Emily," he said in a firm tone. "You've been a bad girl." He shook his head sorrowfully. "To my count, you've broken at least four rules. Not sure you'll survive the punishment for those but, without rules, where would we be? In Armageddon, that's where."

His expression softened. "Tell you what. Since you are my favorite, if you make it alive after you pay your penalty, you can stay out of your cage for at least two hours each day for the next week. Now show yourself."

Abbie sensed an annoying hum behind his words. They had a pull to them. He was using magic to entice Emily out and the girl was responding, for she had moved around to the side. Emily's compliance frightened Abbie more than this fiend's absolute confidence he had the upper hand.

She asked her cord for more information about him.

"His name is Alexander Carlisle," Hafgufa said. *"His ability is like Emily's talent of compulsion, but less powerful."*

That made sense. It would explain how he'd so effectively

tricked Emily into believing his lies and rules. She glanced at Zander, wondering why he hadn't reacted to Hafgufa's words.

"*You didn't broadcast your message?*" Abbie asked, surprised. That would be a first.

"*He means you harm,*" the cord said in a haughty tone.

"Did you transmit to Emily?"

"No, not the children, or they might have given away my presence."

"Good." Abbie suppressed a triumphant smile, impressed by Hafgufa's control at sharing her communications. *"See if you can locate Yousef and let him know that we've located River and I have him in my custody."*

Her cord affirmed she'd sent the message, but said it felt as if she reached across a lake to make contact.

That intrigued Abbie. Since Hafgufa was a deposed water goddess, she would be intimately familiar with movement through bodies of water. She shelved that information for later study and focused on the matter at hand.

Time to end this uncomfortable conversation and get out of here. She aimed her next words at Zander.

"You seem to know me, sir," Abbie said, noting with worry how Zander's intent stare was focused on Emily. Time to shift that focus to herself. "I don't know you. Who are you?"

His gaze swung up to meet hers. He appeared startled, as if he'd forgotten she was still here. "I'm Zander. Emily and River both belong to me. Release them and step back."

"Good to meet you," Abbie said in a chatty tone.

River gave a frightened gasp, and she tightened her hold to show him she had no intention of letting this horrid creature ever take him again.

"You are the one I came to find," she continued. "As for breaking rules, if we circumvented any, it was entirely my fault and I apologize." She pointed to the young girl who now stood just ahead of Abbie, still within invisible Eli, but only a few paces from Zander. "Emily is truly sorry if her absence concerned you. She asked me to bring her back here, which I agreed to do in exchange for her help in finding River."

The child sent a swift, terrified backward glance.

"I've no intention of taking Emily from you," Abbie continued. Then, keeping her gaze fixed on the child, she raised her hand to her heart. "All I came here for is River. Truly."

Emily's eyes widened in surprise and then with acute understanding. She mouthed the word *fib* before she turned to face her captor.

Quick learner.

Abbie dropped her hand and shifted her focus to Zander. "I hope you'll forgive us for coming here so clandestinely, but I seem to have upset Tuuli, so I was avoiding running into her."

He didn't blink at hearing Tuuli's name. A woman he'd nicknamed the she-devil, according to Emily. He'd used the mention of Tuuli to frighten Emily into behaving in the past.

Could she now use Tuuli to frighten him?

Abbie asked her cord, "*What's Zander's relationship with the fae companion?*"

"*He was the first boy taken in this magical child-stealing scheme, thirty-four years and two months ago.*"

That was a stunning bit of information. Just as someone who is abused sometimes becomes the abuser, this abductee had become a serial abductor. Was that what he was doing with Emily? Grooming her to become his successor?

As interesting as this piece of history might be, the revelation hadn't answered her question about his relationship with Tuuli. Or had it?

According to Kiros, nothing happened in the market without Tuuli's knowledge. Abbie went ice cold at all that implied. Had Hafgufa just said that the market's security agent was behind this atrocious child-napping scheme?

"I wasn't trying to steal Emily from you," Abbie said, surprised at how calm she sounded compared to how her stomach churned with a sick feeling. Her mind was feverishly figuring out how she could stop Tuuli if she was behind this long-running crime spree.

She had to be stopped, but was it Abbie's job or Tuuli's siblings' role? If Kiros were to be believed, they may not be aware of Tuuli's child-napping activities. Her immediate concern was getting Emily and River away from this monster.

To distract Zander, she gave Emily a little push toward him, but still left her within Eli's protective but invisible-to-Zander circle. "She's all yours. I'm here strictly for River."

"You can't have the boy," Zander snapped. "You're not his parent and have no rights." His evil smirk left Abbie deeply concerned about Vivian's safety.

"I've been asked by his parents to bring River home," she said, ensuring her cord had a firm grip on Zander's ankle.

"I don't think so," Zander said, absently shaking his left foot. "What's mine stays mine. And no Grimm will say otherwise."

"River was never yours," Abbie replied calmly, "any more than Emily." And she pulled on her cord, with Hafgufa adding a powerful jerk to that action.

He yelped as the cord swept him off his feet. He threw something at Abbie and Eli flared, blinding her. Then flames spewed across the room from her circle. Lucky for Zander, he missed getting scorched because he was flat on his back on the floor as that blazing fire flew over him.

Once the fire died down, Zander asked in a shocked tone, "How did you fend off my attack without a circle?"

She didn't respond, and he grinned. "It's still there, isn't it? You made it invisible."

And now he could tell Tuuli that Abbie had an invisible circle. She sighed in disappointment at losing that advantage.

"You don't know who you're dealing with, Grimm," Zander continued. "You should flee for your life before the she-devil finds you. I've already notified her you're here, so she's likely already on her way."

"Oh, no!" Emily cried out in fear and turned to Abbie.

Abbie held her hand to her heart and said, "I think you're lying."

This coward would never confess to Tuuli that he'd failed. If he did, he would likely end up as her new pair of shoes or, worse, an undergarment.

Walking to the edge of her circle, she used Hafgufa to fling him into the kennel River had been in, and then she locked the door. Only then did she retract her cord back into her arm.

The last time Abbie had confined a prisoner in one of these cages, she'd returned to find the kennel empty. This time, she turned to Emily. "Tell Zander he is not to leave this cage until morning."

That should give them time to get out of this market.

Emily ran over to the kennel's side, unwittingly leaving the circle to do so. Abbie hurried over so the circle could again include the child, and keep her protected.

"Don't you dare!" Zander snarled.

At Abbie's nod, Emily worked her magic.

While she did that, Abbie glanced around the room and noticed further down, two figures crouched within cages, closer to the trapdoor.

Forgetting to stay within Eli, she ran over there, but Eli kept pace with her, bringing Emily and River along, so none of them were ever outside the circle. Once at the other end of the room, Abbie had a better look at the two children in adjacent kennels, sitting quietly, watching her. Neither had lips. The skin on their faces seemed to have grown over their lips.

Behind her, Zander laughed at her horrified gasp.

These must be the two children she spotted being driven away from the hall to the shopping center in Sevenoaks.

"Emily," Abbie said. "Do you know why these two children don't have lips?"

The child glanced over and nodded. "Zander has one of his friends do that to all the new kids. It keeps them quiet until I tell them to not speak."

"Do you know how to release these kids' sealed mouths?" Abbie asked Emily.

The girl shook her head. "The man who does that comes twice a week. If he's been here today, he's not due back for two days." The child glanced up at Abbie with trepidation. "New kids don't eat until he comes to release them. Zander says that's needed to put them in the right frame of mind." She studied the kids. "That's a fib, too, isn't it?"

"Yes, it is," Abbie said. "This is simple cruelty."

"Thanks to you, Grimm, they'll never eat again," Zander shouted at her from his cell. "News has spread that you're in the market. All my men ran away because they knew the she-devil would follow you here. Release me and I'll help you escape."

Abbie ignored his trickery. She wasn't an innocent child to be fooled by his wily words, nor did she need to put her hand to her heart to know this vile villain lied.

She knelt by the first child, a boy about Jimi's age. "I'm going to release you. You'll be home soon."

"How are you going to do that?" Emily asked.

Past Emily, Zander watched them with interest.

Abbie searched the room, then pointed. "Emily, get that blanket from over there and cover Zander's cage."

Emily checked where she pointed and then ran to do as told, moving out of Eli again.

Abbie's heart instantly hammered with fear, but the child was too far away this time to hurry over.

"I can help her," River said, seeing she was worried.

Abbie grabbed his shirt and pulled him back before he, too, stepped out of Eli. "Stay beside me," she warned him. "It's your best protection from being snatched again."

Eyes wide with terror, he nodded his head that he understood.

She kept her cord at the ready to defend Emily if Zander tried anything. She didn't breathe until Emily had draped the cloth over Zander's cage and returned within Eli's protection.

"Don't leave Eli's circle again," Abbie warned Emily, and the girl nodded, paling at the peril she'd been in.

Now they'd blocked Zander's view, Abbie used her cord to unlock the cage and opened the door. The child within scrambled back, looking terrified.

"You're safe," Abbie said in a soothing voice. "I won't hurt you, but I need to break that spell that took away your mouth. Will you let me help?"

The child stared in silence, shivering.

"Nod your head, if it's okay for me to touch you," Abbie said, sliding into the cage.

Once the boy nodded, she inched closer. Hafgufa had pulled part of a spell placed on Figg once and Abbie hoped to repeat that minor miracle.

She sent the cord to wrap around the child's throat and asked her to break the spell placed on this boy to make his mouth vanish.

The cord glowed and sank into the boy's throat. As before, the magic her cord released flowed into Abbie. This time, she was prepared for the influx. It didn't taste as ancient as it had the last time. This felt quite mild in comparison, the magic swirling inside her like a little water sprout looking for an escape hatch.

Abbie forcefully tamped it down. Later, once she was away from this market, she could channel this energy into Klaus, who used such spare magic to pen stories of where the magic originated. Caution kept her from taking that precious book out in public here.

Chapter Thirteen

As Hafgufa unwound the magical spell, the boy's lips took definition, and he dragged in his first deep gasping breath.

"What's your name?" Abbie asked the child.

In answer, he leapt forward to hug Abbie. "I'm Trevor. Thank you!"

Zander swore from within his covered cage and shouted, "How did you free him?"

He must have heard the boy speak.

"Grimms aren't magical," he added, sounding both shocked and a little frightened.

Abbie went over to the adjacent kennel to do the same process with the girl. Once that child was sobbing in Abbie's arms, Eli took the five of them toward the trapdoor.

Her group was getting bigger each moment. She felt like the Pied Piper of Hamelin. Luckily, Eli could expand to transport everyone with no hiccups.

"Wait," Zander shouted. "Don't leave me."

"Be grateful your mouth isn't missing," Abbie said, the energy from the magic from the two spells now residing in her gut trembling to be released. She suspected if she let that magic go, it could shut Zander's lips permanently. Instead, she shut the trapdoor behind her.

Down in the tunnel, Abbie tapped Ruth twice to end the invisibility spell on all of them so Jimi and Nica could give River a hearty welcome. Robert lay slumped on the floor.

"Arthur, can you add your protection to the new children and

Robert?"

"No," her ring replied with sorrow. *"Robert is gravely ill and requires much energy to keep him from slipping away. After helping him, I've just enough to protect you, Jimi, and Nica. The three other children are unprotected."*

"Take your protection off me," Abbie said, now gravely worried about the ghost, *"and add it to keep Robert with us."*

She then warned everyone again to stay within Eli. It was now their best protection. Helping Robert up. "Let's go find Yousef and Vivian and then head home."

"Agreed," he replied, a breathy response that she barely heard. He sounded so ethereal, her heart shuddered with fear he may not make it home.

Briefly, she entertained taking him and the children through the Spell Gate portal first, and returning for the others. Then she reconsidered. What if next time, the Spell Gate gatekeeper refused Abbie's entrance? She'd barely made it through the last time.

As risky as it was to take longer to get home, especially for Robert, it would be better if they all stayed within the safety of Eli. Then they could leave the market together in one fell swoop and never step foot in this place again.

"Do we know where Mrs. Irvine and Mr. Kanaan are located?" Robert asked.

"I suspect they might be in the watery compound," Abbie said, recalling Hafgufa saying she'd reached through a lake to get to Yousef. "If that is so, let's hope Eli, my circle, can take us there without drowning us. Ready?"

Despite everyone's assent, she counted heads before leaving. Six children plus one adult, and one ghost. Check.

"Eli, take us to where Yousef and Vivian are located," Abbie said.

The circle moved along the tunnel for a bit and then, instead of continuing down the corridor, it rose upward. Just as she feared they would all crash into the ceiling, a new tunnel opened up overhead through a ceiling of rock and Eli took them up to the surface. From where they surfaced, he whizzed them across the market toward the watery compound.

"Everyone, take a deep breath and hold it," Abbie warned as, without pause, Eli flew straight into the watery barrier.

Luckily, the circle kept them within an invisible see-through dome that left them with enough air to breathe.

"Wow," Jimi said, as they traveled through what looked like an ocean. He held his hand against the barrier and added, "The water says Vivian and Yousef are here."

"Good," Abbie said.

Eli finally stopped, and she searched for Vivian. Creatures of all shapes and sizes swam closer to look at them, as if Abbie and her group were aquarium specimens.

A large fish rushed up to the edge of their barrier then and spoke directly into her mind. *"How are you here? Circles don't travel outside the marketplace."* At Abbie's shrug, he gave up on that mystery and said, *"We did not invite you. Grimms are forbidden in the market and certainly not permitted to pollute our waters. Leave!"*

Trying not to feel insulted, Abbie introduced herself and said, "We're here to collect two of our missing friends. Do you know where we can find Yousef and Vivian?"

The fish stared at her in silence for a suspenseful moment, his gills moving rapidly as if he were considering how to respond. Then he waved his right fin and a small dome of air rushed up to them with a Siamese cat within it.

Delighted to see the cat, Abbie asked Eli to bring him inside their circle.

"Meow," the cat said on entry as the little dome of air he'd been in dissipated, dropping him.

Thank heavens these fish people hadn't killed Yousef. He looked disgruntled before shaking himself as if to rid water droplets, though he looked perfectly dry. He then rose in a flurry of lights, transforming into his human form dressed in jeans, a light-blue denim shirt, and runners.

Abbie embraced him, thrilled to hold him close. She inhaled his scent–a combination of plum, currant, and an unknown woodsy trace, with an undercurrent of jasmine. He always smelled so good and a little exotic. She was certain she could identify each of her friends by scent alone. Jimi and Nica, each had a unique perfume that perfectly reflected their personality and background, as did the others.

"I'm so glad you're safe, Yousef," she said.

"You, too!" He held her a moment before pulling back to glance at the children crowding her circle. "Been collecting friends, have we?" he asked with a tolerant smile. "Including River! We were worried about you, young man."

"He has been brave," Robert said.

Yousef glanced at the ghost, his cheerful smile fading. "Anything I can do to help you, my lord?"

"The sooner we leave this market, the better," Abbie replied quietly as Robert shook his head.

River turned to Yousef. "Abbie said you came here with my mum. Where is she?"

Abbie laid a gentle hand on the boy's tense shoulder. "We're about to find out." She faced the fish that looked like a lake trout. "Where is Vivian?"

"She's not your business," the fish replied. *"We've returned the interloper cat. Now leave."*

"We're not going anywhere without her," Abbie said.

The fish swam around her circle until he came closer to Robert. *"If you stay much longer, that one won't survive to make it back to your realm. Best go now."*

"No," Robert said, in a remarkably firm tone. "We will not be leaving without this boy's mother."

"Mother?" the fish said, sounding shocked. *"Are you her missing boy?"*

"You told her you knew where her son was," Yousef said in a dark tone. "That's why she stayed, to free him. I should have eaten you when I had the chance. I still might."

Yousef snapped his teeth, and the fish backed up in a hurry.

Abbie refrained from telling Mr. Trout that Yousef was a vegan and that last was an idle threat.

The fish swam closer. If it were human, Abbie suspected it would have been smirking. "You can't enter our waters."

"Yes, we can," Jimi said, and pulled out his sword.

Before Abbie could shout, "No!" the boy struck with his weapon and cleaved the barrier that separated them from the water. A deluge poured in, sweeping them all off their feet.

The kids screamed.

"Take us out of here," Abbie shouted to Eli, who instantly took them to the other side of the water barrier.

Water drained out, and they all lay down, soaked and coughing out liquid. They were on a street in the market, outside the water compound.

"Sorry," Jimi said, the first to speak.

"Well," Abbie said, "now we know the sword works. I didn't think anything could tear through a circle's defense barrier."

"Where is your circle?" Yousef asked, rising and looking around. "I lost mine as soon as I entered that watery grave."

Hers was still invisible to everyone but her and her kids. At least Ruth's spell still held. She was about to ask the mirror to make Eli visible again when, on impulse, she changed her mind. At least until Eli had recovered from the tearing Jimi had given him.

The circle probably needed all his spare energy to heal. She knelt to place her hand on Eli. "Are you alright?"

"Yes," he responded in a gentle voice. *"I am unharmed. The boy tore me in two. Once we left that watery environment, I resealed myself. I have also strengthened my barriers so that will not happen again. Do you wish to return to the water realm?"*

Good question. "Shall we try again to reach Vivian?" Abbie asked her soaked crew. "Everyone up for another trip into the water compound?"

Before they could answer, someone dropped out of the water barrier. Vivian landed on her feet in front of Abbie.

"You're safe," she said in relief at seeing Vivian and hand Eli include her inside the circle.

Vivian's gaze zeroed in on her son.

"River!" she cried and opened her arms.

"Mama." The boy ran into his mother's hold and burst into tears.

Over her son's shoulder, Vivian mouthed the words *"thank*

you" to Abbie, her eyes filled with grateful tears.

Suddenly, a commotion occurred between all the kids. Nica and Jimi were shouting. When she turned back to see what the problem was, her kids pointed across the street.

"We tried to hold her, but she pulled away," Jimi said. "We didn't leave Eli, like you asked, so we couldn't stop her."

Abbie moved the kids apart and realized who was missing. Emily.

The child was up the street and inside Zander's circle with another man beside them. The child turned and Abbie's heart squeezed in terror to see Emily's mouth sealed.

When Jimi sliced Eli in two, that must have temporarily broken her circle's protection over all of them, including Emily. And while Abbie's worry for Eli and her joy at being reunited with Vivian distracted her, Zander must have exploited that opening to snatch the child. His mouth-sealing friend must have helped him escape from the kennel she'd trapped him in.

She raised her arm to shoot her cord to grab Emily when, beside her, Robert groaned and collapsed. She barely caught him, kneeling to cradle Robert's head.

By the time she glanced back, it was too late. Emily was gone.

If Abbie hadn't been kneeling, holding onto Robert, she would have collapsed, too. Her legs were trembling with horror that she'd lost Emily. She wanted to rush off to find the child, but couldn't delay taking Robert home any longer or she'd lose him, too. Getting her kids out of this market was also as important as saving Robert.

"We have to get him home now," she said with finality.

Together, she and Yousef raised Robert to his feet. She

then tapped her mirror once to hide herself and everyone in her party. Abbie then asked Eli to speed them to the car park outside the market.

As they traveled, zipping past stalls, her mind spun with plans on what to do next. First, she had some news for Vivian. "Your husband was hurt before we left Earth. You'll need to check on him when you get home."

Hugging her son, Vivian gave her a startled glance. Then she shut her eyes, a frown on her forehead. When she snapped her eyes open, she said, "He's in a hospital in Kent. I can see him clearly because there's a glass of water beside him. He has a gash on the side of his head, but he seems alert."

"Wow," Abbie said. That was quite the water talent.

Vivian gave her a look of curiosity. "How did you get into the Spell Gate market?"

"Long story," Abbie said. "Do you know who was behind you being snatched and why?"

The woman hesitated; her gaze evasive. Finally, she murmured, "I may have misled you about who I am."

"Who are you?" Yousef asked Vivian. "After the water people snatched us, they incarcerated me in water! Luckily, our captors were like dogs–no sense at all–so I escaped and tried to find you. I deserve an honest answer."

Her guilty gaze flew to meet his. "Thank you for that rescue attempt. And I am grateful to all of you for saving River. I won't forget what you've done for my family."

Abbie nodded. "Would who you are have something to do with why Jimi's plastic sword could cut through our watery surrounds?"

Vivian's gaze met Abbie's, and she smiled. "You are clever.

I am a Lady of the Lake. The water community wanted me to return to the duties I gave up when I married Seamus. They promised to release River if I would agree. Except they didn't have him."

"No," Abbie said, astounded by Vivian's admission. Could she mean Lady of the Lake as in King Arthur's court? It explained River's water talent. And Jimi's sword, Caleb. Related to the fabled Excalibur?

"Will you do as the water people ask," Abbie asked, "despite them lying to you?"

"I'm considering it," Vivian said, with a slight up tilt of her lips. "Being in that watery compound reminded me how much I'd missed my true home environment."

"I want to come, too," River said. "Can I?"

"We'll talk it over with your dad," she promised.

Eli now sped them all toward the market's entrance. As they passed the guard, he started, eyes opening wide with surprise. Since Abbie, her friends, and Eli were invisible, she suspected he must somehow have sensed their passage.

Abbie asked Eli to head to Vivian's car first.

Her precious time with her friends and family had ended. When they came to a halt, Vivian stepped out of Eli with River.

Now everyone was safe and heading home, Abbie tapped Ruth twice to turn off the invisibility spell.

"Vivian, I'd like you to take these two children with you." Abbie shepherded the two she'd found in the cages out of Eli. "Once home, please see if you can find their parents and reunite them."

"Will do." Vivian took Abbie's hand and squeezed it before she leaned in. "You're staying, aren't you?"

Abbie nodded. "Watch over my friends and family, too?"

"Count on it." She then ushered the two kids now in her care into her back seat and River into the front passenger side. Then she waved goodbye to everyone else. "See you in Kent."

Eli next brought Yousef, Robert, Abbie, and her kids to a halt beside Rosie. This time, the parking spot beside them was empty, giving them room to spread out. As the kids left Eli, their smaller circle vanished.

Just as she suspected. The kids' circle had only remained active while it remained within Eli, who could travel outside the market.

Abbie handed Yousef her car keys. "I'd like you to drive Robert, Nica, and Jimi home."

"You're going to find Emily," Nica accused.

Abbie addressed Nica and Jimi directly. "I shouldn't be long. If I am delayed, for any reason, you have the rest of the Standard Bearers' group and my mother to watch over you two until I return. Vivian has also promised to help when needed."

She gently shifted a stray lock of dark hair off Nica's solemn face. "Emily has no one but me to help her, love, and I promised I would take her to her mother."

"I want to help," Nica cried and hugged Abbie tight.

Jimi joined his sister. "Me, too."

"Thank you," Abbie said, holding them close and cherishing the wonderful feeling of having them safely in her arms. "This once, I'd like you two to do as I say. Just as I have another Standard Bearer job to do with Emily, your SB job will be to ensure Robert reaches St. Michael's safely."

She pulled back so she could look at their little faces. "Will you do this for me?"

"But I can help you," Jimi said, bursting into tears. "I know I can."

Abbie played her last card. "Robert needs you more."

Yousef nodded. "I came here to find you two, and I'm not leaving without you."

Abbie sent him a grateful glance. "You two need to guard Yousef as he takes Robert to St. Michael's as soon as possible to save him. He has to be your top priority."

Yousef settled Robert in Rosie's front seat and then held the back door open for the kids.

Nica and Jimi glanced from Abbie to Robert and she could see the horrible choice they felt they must make. Then Jimi took his sister's hand and drew her into the back seat. Nica followed reluctantly, her tearful gaze never leaving Abbie.

"How will you get back?" Yousef asked.

Her gaze swept the now fairly empty car park and landed on Zander's dark hatchback. "I've got a plan," she said.

He nodded, but looked as unhappy as her kids when he entered the driver's seat. Abbie stepped back. The gatekeeper's claws settled over Rosie to transport the vehicle and its occupants back to Earth.

Her children watched her from the car window while Robert slumped against the passenger window up front. Then Rosie shimmered as the Spell Gate opened to take them home. In the blink of an eye, the car vanished.

Satisfied her kids were on their safe way home, Abbie tapped Ruth once and then said to Eli, "Take me to Emily."

Her circle didn't move.

Worried at Eli's unresponsiveness, Abbie knelt and laid her right hand on the circle. "Why are we not moving?"

"I cannot sense where she is," Eli replied.

Her first terrified thought was that Zander had killed the child. She squashed that unconfirmed concern. Zander had wanted Emily back badly, so he must consider her too valuable to destroy. She was safe. Somewhere.

"Can you sense Zander?"

Eli was silent a moment, searching. Then the circle said, *"Yes, but his essence is faint and fading fast."*

Was he hiding, too? With no more time to spare, Abbie asked Eli to take her to him. Now! Wherever he was, Emily should be nearby. If she wasn't, her cord could get him to talk.

Soon, Abbie lost sight of the car park behind her as she approached the market entrance columns. The guard still couldn't see her since she and Eli were invisible, but the fluttering of his shirt at her swift passage had him swinging around with a grave face.

Out of curiosity, Abbie glanced up. Only the back end of the giant griffin statues greeted her sight. No sign of the angel. She released a sigh of disappointment.

Eli took her inside the tunnel and stopped beneath the trapdoor. Someone had locked it and she sensed a spell over the door to prevent it from being opened.

Her cord broke through that magical barrier in a snap. She flicked on the light in the tunnel, but stayed put, giving herself time to adjust to the change in lighting. While she waited, Abbie asked Arthur to raise her shield to maximum strength and primed her cord to strike.

Finally, taking a deep breath for courage, she opened the trapdoor and rose into the kennel room.

The rectangular space was lit and empty of people. No, not

quite empty. There were two men here, Zander and the man she'd seen earlier. The cloth Emily had used to cover a cage lay discarded. The men were inside two adjacent cages.

Eli slid her forward to where both men lay curled in their individual prisons, dead eyes wide open, mouths sealed shut. Even the one whom she thought possessed that talent had his mouth sealed.

Whoever had placed them in here must have had this poor fellow seal his own mouth shut, then killed him and Zander. That senseless cruelty left her dumbfounded and shivering with dread for Emily's safety.

This must be why Eli had trouble tracking Zander. He hadn't been going into hiding. He'd been dying.

An icy chill swept down Abbie's spine as she swung around to see if anyone watched her. The room was eerily empty.

Chapter Fourteen

If these two murders were Tuuli's handiwork–who else could it have been but Zander's *she-devil*–she must be in a foul mood.

Was Emily still alive?

If she was dead, she would have been in another cage, like those two sorry souls. That meant she could be with Tuuli. But why would she take the child?

The fae companion must know Abbie would notify her immortal siblings of what she had been up to at the Spell Gate market. If she believed Abbie had become attached to Emily, she could have taken her as insurance.

To keep me quiet?

Or to bait a Grimm trap?

Not wanting to see the two contorted dead men any longer, she picked up the covering off the floor and draped it over the two cages. Then, taking a deep shuddering breath, since her legs were ready to give way, she slumped inside the hovering circle, her back to the row of cages.

Before she faced Tuuli, she had to do some thinking about her next move. Since Eli only needed to transport her, he had shrunk closer to her. Abbie touched the circle. "Can you still not sense Emily?"

"No."

"Has she left the market?" Abbie asked, frowning.

"Emily is in this realm, but I do not know where."

Odd. Abbie had thought these circles could take her to anyone she wanted to visit. As head of security, could Tuuli have hidden Emily from a circle's ability to sense her?

"Can you sense where Tuuli is?"

"No." After a brief hesitation, Eli added, *"She, too, is still within this realm. She and Emily are together. But I cannot sense their exact location."*

Interesting. The gatekeeper that transported her friends home could have notified Tuuli that the Grimm had stayed behind. Could that knowledge have sent Tuuli into clean-up mode? And now into hiding? Or was Tuuli stalling for time while she called up reinforcements? Would her siblings come to her aid as Oliver had said, if she termed this an emergency?

Kiros told her earlier this year that he believed a Grimm would be his and his siblings' doom. That's why they were desperate to make that peace pact with her. Today, the food vendor had said Grimms were forbidden in the Spell Gate market because a prophecy said a Grimm entering would bring about the time of battle. In a market where an immortal companion was in charge of security. Coincidence? She no longer believed in that.

A battle between her and Tuuli was indeed brewing, but was it about to lead to one between Abbie and all immortal companions? If so, she wasn't ready. All she had at her command was her cord, which couldn't kill, and Arthur, who'd been pushed to his limits today. And her angel-touched circle. The rest of her Grimm artifacts, except for Ruth and Klaus, were back in Kent, as were the other Standard Bearers.

This was now her fight alone.

A warm wind blew at her side. She sprang to her feet. After checking the origin of the air movement, she swung around toward the trapdoor. Cautiously, cord fully drawn out, she had

Eli take her to that opening and she peered into the hole.

Nica and Jimi glanced back up at her.

Abbie's legs gave way for the second time and she slumped to the floor, stunned. How could they still be here? The gatekeeper had taken Rosie away with them inside the car.

Taking a calming breath, she waited quietly, heart pounding with dread, as the children rose to the kennel room with a new circle.

"You two are grounded forever!" Abbie said in a voice ridden by fear.

Holding her brother's hand, Nica brought them closer to Eli and knelt in front of Abbie. "I'm never letting you go again," Nica said in a quiet, determined tone.

"She means it," Jimi said in a grave voice. "I don't mind anymore, so you might as well not, too."

Abbie was speechless for several moments. Finally, she voiced her most pressing concern. "What about Robert?"

"Yousef's taken him home," Nica said. "Jimi told the gatekeeper that we had to stay here to save you and Emily because we love you, but that Robert needed to return to Earth right away or he'd die. So, it dropped Rosie with Yousef and Robert home and placed us back in the market."

"I also asked Rosie to not open her doors to anyone," Jimi added in a solemn tone, "until they reached St. Michael's. So, they will be safe."

"Of course you did," Abbie said, half exasperated, and half impressed by their ingenuity. At least Robert was on his way to St. Michael's where he could recover. One worry off her list. "Where did you get your new circle?"

"The entrance guard gave it to us after we said you needed

our help," Nica said. "He asked us to tell you that when the fighting starts, to remember that he helped us, too."

Abbie was still shaking in disbelief. Sitting in front of her, their circle butting Eli, each child took one of her hands.

At their touch, she realized her kids had done what she hadn't been able to do lately. She'd been preaching to her SB crew to not run from trouble since her mother tricked Abbie into avoiding the catastrophe of the London bus blowing up.

Yet, all she'd wanted since she lost her kids at that recital hall in Sevenoaks was to find Nica, Jimi, and friends and run to safety. Until someone took Emily.

Even then, she faced adversity alone, instead of with her SB crew. It was as if she'd reverted to the young woman she'd been after the devastation of losing her friends to the bus bombing. Thinking she had no one else to rely on but herself.

Yet, she was no longer that traumatized woman. She, her kids, and her four friends were firmly bonded as Standard Bearers. What had begun as a game to distract these two little ones from their grief had grown into a calling. One where, not just Abbie, but *all of them,* had promised to defend the weak. How could she have forgotten that?

She kissed Nica and Jimi's hands, her throat choked with emotions, unable to voice how glad she was to see them. Despite being children, her kids were as much Standard Bearers as Judith, Talin, Yousef, and herself.

Abbie met and held Jimi's gaze. Like her, Jimi, too, sometimes acted as if he must solve his problems alone. Where had he picked up that bad habit? From her? Kids learn by watching adults.

She recalled Nica's breakdown when Abbie left her kids

behind to go back in time with Judith to recover her friend's gran. She'd consoled Nica and promised to return. Jimi had cried, but he hadn't reacted as emotionally as his sister.

Yet, could that moment have taught him that sometimes, each of them needed to act on their own? Then COVID had hit, and she'd had to separate from her kids again, this time for months. That last experience might have cemented Jimi's belief that he only had himself to rely on. If so, it was time she dissuaded him of that concept.

"No more running off alone to save a friend," she said in a firm tone to Jimi. "For any of us. We're Standard Bearers who have each other to lean on in hard times. Right?"

He frowned a moment, as if considering her words.

"I should have asked you two to help me save Emily," Abbie admitted, wanting to teach Jimi how a team should act. "That's what Standard Bearers do. We work together to solve our cases."

"Does this mean you're not mad?" Jimi asked.

"You came to me," Abbie said. "I could never be mad about that. But when you set out on an adventure, it would be better to have an adult accompany you."

Jimi's tense shoulders relaxed, as if a huge load had dropped off his shoulders. "We had Robert with us."

Abbie nodded. "But Robert almost died because he felt he had to follow you here to protect you."

His face solemn, Jimi said, "Abbie."

"Yes?" she asked.

"I'm sorry for hiding in that man's car at the recital hall with Nica. When I learned from the house where he was going, I should have told you, and then we could have figured out how to follow him."

"Thank you for saying that, Jimi," Abbie said with deep sincerity.

Jimi held out his fist.

A wave of calm washed over her at the familiar gesture that always evoked a celestial blessing on their current mission.

His sister touched her fist to his.

Abbie joined hers to theirs.

Klaus flew out of her bra and landed on the floor, expanding beneath their fists. He opened his pages and light poured out of the book, highlighting their fists.

"Ooh," Jimi said in awe. "That feels hot."

Then, one by one, Abbie sensed Yousef, Talin, and Judith, and finally, even Robert's fists join theirs. It was as if Klaus had unlocked a portal to allow her friends to join in on this ceremony.

The weight of their friends' support flowed into Abbie. Jimi and Nica gasped, suggesting they, too, had felt that amazing connection. In that instant, a flash sparked and a spear of light soared from their joined fist bump, shooting straight toward the ceiling. Euphoria lightened Abbie's spirit.

Finally, they drew back their fists, and the light died down. Klaus shut his cover, shrank back to his tiny version, and flew into Abbie's bra. *"Thank you for helping us connect with our friends,"* she said silently to the book and gave it a gentle pat.

The book settled more comfortably, as if pleased by her acknowledgment.

Her hand tingling, she met her children's equally stunned expressions. All their hands still glowed.

"I feel different," Nica said in wonder. "Like the other

Standard Bearers are inside me."

"Me, too," Jimi said, sounding surprised.

Could their SB connection be lingering even after their fist bump ended? She did feel odd. As if she were full of magic. Was it merely the energy she'd absorbed earlier when she released the spells on the two children she'd found here?

"I feel like I could be a cat," Jimi said. The moment he said the words, he changed into a black, short-haired feline.

"Oh!" Nica cried in surprise. "I feel as if I have Talin's electricity coursing through me." She pointed to a switch on the wall and the room went dark and, a moment later, the overhead lights turned back on.

Abbie frowned at the black cat and Nica's straight black hair, which now looked as if it had received a bad perm.

Nica had Talin's electromagnetic talent, and Jimi had gained Yousef's shape-shifting ability. Could she have Judith's Taoist magic? Was that the foreign power coursing through her? She held her fingers the way she'd seen her friend do the first day she returned to Chipstead, Kent. Abbie circled her hand over Nica's feet and Jimi's paws.

"Try to move," she told the kids.

"I can't!" Nica cried. "I'm stuck to the floor."

Jimi mewed in protest and then sat down on his hind legs, his fur standing up on his back and his tail bushy.

Abbie released them. "I have Judith's ability."

Jimi snapped back to his human form and asked, "What about Robert?"

"He might be too weak to transfer his ghostly ability to us," Abbie said. "But let's test out that theory." She stood and asked Eli to take her toward the closest wall that didn't have iron in it. In no time, she moved through a back wall into an adjacent room full of storage boxes. She returned, grinning.

"Can we do everyone's magic?" Nica asked.

"No," Abbie said. "It was Eli who walked through that wall and took me along. I think Robert's talent went into my circle, but we can check." She pictured Yousef in his cat form and said, "I want to be a Siamese cat." Nothing changed. "So, no, we don't have everyone's talent. But this changes everything."

"What do you mean?" Nica asked.

"It means we're not alone in this fight. The full Standard Bearers crew is here in the market. And we have a wicked enemy to face down. Tuuli. Eli says that she has Emily. Tuuli is powerful and scary. She's killed two people so far. We need to get Emily away from her before she hurts her. If we're to rescue her, we need to act as a team."

She asked Eli to bring in the two kids and their circle, and then she faced her children. "Before we set off on this rescue, I want you both to promise to stay within Eli at all times. It was because Emily stepped beyond this circle's protection that her enemies could take her. Will you both do as I ask and never leave Eli's protection?"

The two children nodded vigorously.

"Yes, I promise," Nica said.

"Me, too," Jimi said.

This time Abbie did as she'd taught Emily. She put her hand to her heart and shut her eyes. Something deep inside her said the kids meant what they said this time. She sighed in profound relief and opened her eyes. It was good to be on the same footing with these two.

"We're the Standard Bearers," Jimi began.

"We save those in dire need," Nica finished.

Abbie nodded, and added, "Together."

She then tapped Ruth once. Once that invisibility spell was active, she said, "Time to retrieve Emily."

"Where is she?" Nica asked.

"Unknown," Abbie admitted. "Let's return to the fae forest compound and speak to Oliver. He seemed canny about how the market and its magical defenses work. He might help us locate Tuuli's whereabouts. Ready?" At the kids' acknowledgment, Abbie said, "Eli, take us to Oliver."

Her circle instantly whizzed them down into the tunnel and before long, brought them up to the fae section. She turned, expecting to find Oliver, but directly before them was a wide gray stump easily the size of a small room.

She shivered and pulled her kids closer as a terrible certainty washed over her. This was all that was left of the yew tree. Absolute silence bathed the forest, as if every fae creature whose light Abbie had seen the last time she visited had gone into hiding.

Tuuli had beaten them here. With Oliver sadly gone, if there were fae here who might help, she needed them to see her. Abbie tapped her mirror twice to turn off the spell.

Jimi pulled out of her hold and moved closer toward the tree stump, dragging Nica with him, who still refused to let go of her brother's hand. Abbie watched with a troubled frown.

Ever since River was first taken, her boy had acted recklessly. Though he had good instincts and a powerful magical talent, they had reached a perilous stage in their mission to retrieve Emily. She needed Jimi to think and act in the best interest of all of them, not simply react to his needs.

It was unsafe for either him or Nica to leave Eli's protection, as she had warned in the kennel room. Jimi had promised to listen to her. Was he about to disobey her again?

She clenched her fists to stop the instinctive motherly response of dragging Jimi and his sister back, either physically or by using her cord. Instead, Abbie simply waited.

Please help him to trust me to lead him, she prayed.

Just as she needed her kids to trust her, she, too, had to trust her kids to be sensible when outside forces distracted her, as they had when Zander took Emily. Jimi and Nica were old enough to remember to not cross the street without looking both ways. To not touch a hot stove. To listen when she said, *Do not step outside Eli.*

Jimi stopped at the edge of Eli's circle and sent her a pleading glance. "Please, may I get closer to Oliver?"

Abbie released a pent-up breath of profound relief. "Well done, Jimi," she said, overwhelmed with pride. "Thank you for asking for my help. That means the world to me."

A small smile lit his face at her compliment. The first one she had seen on him since Zander kidnapped River.

She then instructed Eli to move forward with all of them, so Jimi could reach what remained of Oliver.

The boy leaned forward and gently stroked the thick flaky gray stump, and frowned with concentration. He seemed to commune with what was left of this giant, ancient tree.

When Jimi turned back, his eyes were teary. "I can feel Oliver inside the stump, Abbie, but he's weak. He can't speak."

Abbie touched the stump herself and asked her cord if she could help revive this dying tree.

"His life spark has withered too much," Hafgufa said in a

sorrowful tone. *"The spell that felled him cannot be undone. If I try, it would kill him instantly."*

Abbie hugged Jimi and Nica close, a terrible anger brewing. There had been no reason for this slaughter other than pure vindictiveness. She was certain Oliver had been attacked only because he'd helped Abbie. She feared now for the other two in this market who had helped her–the guard at the entrance and the food stall attendant.

Carlos Ortiz had given her kids their new circle, so he must still be alive. Hopefully, Jakka, the food seller, had quit the market before Tuuli reached her. She was about to turn away from the stump when a better idea occurred.

Abbie pulled out the magic stones Carlos had gifted her. "I wonder if these wish stones, augmented by the magic Hafgufa shunted into me and Judith's Taoist energy, might be enough to revive Oliver?"

"Oh, please let's try," Nica said. "I'll help with what Talin gave me of his electromagnetic magic. Maybe that can give Oliver the extra life spark he needs to live again."

Jimi stood on his tiptoes to look at the stones Abbie held. "They say they work when the user imagines something and then tosses them into the air."

Abbie nodded. "That helps, Jimi, thank you. Let's give this a try." Abbie shut her eyes, picturing Oliver as he had once been. Then Abbie spun the power that had been agitating within her for release into the stones. Judith's Taoist magic, with its oriental flavor, mingled in as well. Then she flung the three colorful stones high above the stump.

The wish stones sparked and flared, bright as the sun, encompassing the entire trunk. Nica pointed to the trunk and instantly, clouds thundered above, flashing and raining lightning rods toward the tree stump.

Abbie told Eli to hurry them away so they wouldn't get scorched by the energy that flew in the air around the flare engulfing the stump.

Once the thunder quieted and the flare faded away, where the gray stump had been, now stood a thick giant red-brown trunk that was sky high. Tall, healthy, and alive.

"Wow," Nica whispered.

For once, even Jimi appeared speechless.

Abbie couldn't contain her glee, but was this still their Oliver or a brand-new tree?

"Oliver?" she called up. "Are you back?"

"Yes, I'm back," his familiar voice boomed. *"But how?"*

"With a little help from friends," she said, grinning widely. She couldn't help herself. It felt so good to see Oliver back in excellent form. "Oliver, we hate to save and dash, but we came because we need your help. Tuuli's taken the little girl that was with me earlier. Do you know how we can find out where she is being held?"

Chapter Fifteen

Oliver was silent a moment as he contemplated Abbie's request. Finally, he asked, "Are you certain you wish to cross the evil queen?"

A valid question from someone who'd just recovered from being brutally attacked by Tuuli. Also, Abbie felt the absence of magic within herself after she'd used that energy to save the tree. She'd have to check with Nica later if she felt the same loss of Talin's magic. If so, that only left Yousef and Robert's magic at their disposal. But at least now, with Oliver revived, they might find out where Emily was being held.

"I promised Emily that I would take her back to her mother," she said to the yew tree, "and I mean to do that. She's had so many broken promises in her young life, you see. I cannot add to her list of betrayals."

"Very well," he said. "But it'll require more help to find her. She's hiding, but she cannot evade all of us."

"All of whom?" Abbie asked, frowning.

Oliver stomped one of his low-lying branches and it shook the ground. Abbie hung onto her kids until the ground stopped trembling. Eli rose higher, not to be disturbed.

Soon, little lights appeared all around the tree. Oliver looked as if he were conversing with them and then they all flew away in different directions.

"I've put out a call to everyone in the market," Oliver said. "If anyone sees or has seen Queen Tuuli, they will notify me. Never fear, we will find her."

Oliver's network was spread out efficiently across the

market. He seemed certain everyone would cooperate. To help a Grimm! A person to whom the market had forbidden entrance.

Abbie had to ask. "Why would they want to help me?"

If a tree could ever be said to shrug, this one did. "In the short time you've been with us, you re-united the Lady of the Lake with the water community. Demolished the child-snatching net that has plagued the human-supes for decades." He spread his branches wide and bowed. "Even brought a fae back from the brink of death. If nothing else, they do not wish to make an enemy of you."

He straightened and stood still, as if listening. Then he said, "Found her, but going to double-check this." He paused and spoke to a grayish light that zipped closer. "Hmm..."

"What's wrong?" Abbie asked.

"Queen Tuuli is where fae never enter," he said in a ponderous tone. "But fae have friends from that dark realm who love to gossip. I know exactly where she is."

"Where's that?" Abbie asked, certain she wasn't going to like the answer.

"In the underworld compound."

"That makes sense," Abbie said, even as deep dread rose within her at having to enter there. "Kiros, her human sibling, said she and their underworld bro are close. I can see her going to his people for help if she was in trouble."

Abbie's grip on her kids tightened. Tuuli's underworld sibling was no friend to her or the Standard Bearers. That fiend had single-handedly killed many Grimms. Vulcan had also sent a demon to kill the kids' mother and arranged for the London bombing.

The underworld companion was the reason she couldn't stomach agreeing to Kiros's "let bygones be bygones" proposal. If anything could have dissuaded her from going after Tuuli, it was this news. Yet, she couldn't leave Emily in that fae companion's clutches.

Oliver held out a branch. "Should your kiddies stay with me while you go? I can ensure they stay safe here."

"No, you said we work as a team," Nica said.

"Together," Jimi added.

Abbie couldn't bring herself to let them out of her sight while they were off-world, anyway. Her Grimm instincts also shouted they were safer within Eli, an angel-blessed circle, than anywhere else.

There was a way to verify that last assumption was correct. "Nica, do you still have any of Talin's magic left?"

The child's lips pressed tight, as if she didn't want to admit what Abbie already suspected.

"We need to know what we're going in with," Abbie said. "I have little left of Judith's magic."

"Yousef's ability is still in me," Jimi said.

"Talin's electromagnetic energy is all gone," Nica admitted. "It was all used up to help Oliver. Sorry, Abbie."

"Don't be," Abbie said. "If you hadn't given your whole heart into saving Oliver, I doubt we'd even have a lead to where Emily is being held." She hugged the girl tight. "What this confirms is that we're safer within Eli than without. Tuuli almost killed Oliver." She then said to the yew tree, "Thanks for the offer, but they'll both be coming with me."

The kids relaxed.

Oliver nodded, his branches adjusting to give an

impression of sadness and concern at her decision. "Very well," he said, and gave her directions on where to find Tuuli. "The instant you enter that compound, they'll identify you."

"Why is that?" Abbie asked.

"Because, first, no one other than underworld folk enters there, though demons travel to our sites often enough. Second, you're all colorful."

Abbie frowned at that last odd reason, but she had a plan to get in and out, hopefully without alerting Tuuli. All she wanted was Emily. She still leaned toward allowing the other immortal companions to deal with Tuuli.

She tapped her mirror once to start the invisibility spell.

The moment the spell activated, Oliver said, "Oh ho! That's how you plan to sneak into the underworld. You are a crafty one, Grimm. But the kids' little circle is still visible."

"Right." She'd forgotten about that. But maybe that was just as well. Since they were no longer in the market proper, she bet if that smaller circle moved out of Eli, it would fade away. She asked the kids to step out of it and then had Eli eject it. When he did, the little circle vanished.

Good. One less item to keep track of.

"Best of luck," Oliver called out as Eli zipped them off. "You're going to need it, Grimm."

Abbie and her kids were soon passing several encampments. They'd seen some earlier, from the human-supe faction to water folks, and even a celestial zone. They finally arrived at a location that looked as if it was twilight. Despite all the other locations basking under daylight, this section looked like nighttime approached.

"It's all gray," Jimi said.

"Even the trees," Nica said, shifting herself between Jimi and Abbie so she could hold both their hands.

The children were correct. Everything in this underworld compound was in shades of gray. The temperature was also uncomfortably hot and the air stank of sulfur and other odious scents. To the creatures who lived here, she and her kids–who were painfully colorful–likely also stank of what could be a malodorous scent to them. She hoped that wouldn't alert anyone to their passage.

Unlike the fishy inhabitants in the water compound, demons and monsters dwelled here. All looked quite ferocious. Yet, they behaved like ordinary folks. They went about their business, stopping to shop at stalls or eat odd-looking things that squeaked in terror when chomped on.

Abbie hoped she or her kids wouldn't end up on one of these creatures' plates.

The only demon Abbie had met before today was the one at St. Michael's graveyard and he'd appeared red-skinned. Perhaps they took on a more colorful appearance when they left their home domain.

She placed a finger to her lips to show she wanted everyone to remain silent while they were here. Both children nodded, fear clear on their faces.

Eli then took them toward a mountainous region and a structure that looked to be a large, elaborately carved gray mansion. Etched out of the side of a mountain, the building's rear was buried in rock. Two horned gray demons guarded the enormous front doors.

Despite having passed several demons on her way here, she shivered at the sight of those guards. She couldn't help remembering that according to Klaus, Tuuli's brother had often used demons to kill Grimms. Did Tuuli now plan to use her brother's tactic to be rid of her Grimm problem? Is that why she was hiding out in this underworld encampment?

Nica's hold on Abbie tightened, and she squeezed the child's hand to offer what little comfort her touch could give.

Abbie urged Eli to explore all sides of the house for signs of occupation. They peeked into windows, but most chambers were shuttered and dark, as if this were an abandoned home. Only two rooms showed elves, pixies, and other winged fae creatures frantically cleaning.

It was as if the owner had returned unexpectedly and the place had to be readied. If the fae avoided this underworld region, Tuuli must have compelled them to come here.

Despite her servants being here, Tuuli and Emily weren't in any of the rooms visible from the outside. Time to head inside. When she asked Eli to do that, he stayed put.

"What's the matter?" she asked the circle.

"This abode is magically protected."

Abbie was about to pull out her cord to see if she could dismantle the barrier spell when Jimi spoke.

"Robert could enter Granny Chan's home even though she'd spelled it to keep out everyone but you and us."

Of course! Robert's ability had transferred to the circle after their fist bump. "Eli, you shouldn't need an opening in the barrier to enter. Try to go straight in."

The circle hesitated and then moved closer to the house and then sailed inside.

They entered a shuttered room on the ground floor. Then they traveled through several adjacent chambers in the back of the house that didn't look as if anyone had visited in ages. Before long, they came across a kitchen, which was a bright gray room with a head demon cook and nervous fae helpers busy preparing a meal.

Despite tentacles and limbs hanging out of pots, the flavorful scents were alarmingly tempting. She must be hungry.

Not finding Emily on the bottom floor, they headed upstairs. In a large chamber on the left wing of the third floor, they spotted Tuuli reposing on a pale pink divan. She slept while fae servants tip-toed around her, cleaning and straightening the room.

Since they couldn't see Emily in here, Abbie urged Eli to quit the room and check the adjoining chambers. Finally, they reached the landing of the top floor, which looked to be the attic. The ceiling was low here, with only a few rooms. They checked all of them. None were occupied. Disappointed, they returned to the landing by the stairs.

Abbie sat, frustration and fear warring within her. "She has to be here somewhere."

The kids slumped beside her.

She double-checked with Eli, who insisted Emily was in this house, but he could not identify where.

"Abbie, should I ask the house?" Jimi asked.

She glanced at him in surprise. Usually, he spoke to things without asking her permission. She was glad he was being more cautious, but had to ask, "Why are you hesitating?"

He shrugged. "Everything here feels wrong. As if things aren't right in their minds. I think if I ask the house, it might tell on us to Tuuli that we're here."

"Good point," Abbie agreed. "Better not to ask then. But

maybe my cord can help us. Hafgufa, can you find out where Emily is in this house without alerting Tuuli?"

Her cord slid out of her finger and wrapped around one of the stair railings. *"She is in the room you visited earlier. Where Tuuli was resting. Emily is the pink Divan."*

If her kids weren't with her, Abbie would have sworn. Of course! Tuuli had changed Emily's form. Not into clothes or shoes this time, but into furniture. One she rested on, so Abbie couldn't steal her and slink away.

"What are we going to do now, Abbie?" Nica asked.

She hugged her daughter close. "No choice but for me to confront Tuuli." Abbie took a deep breath and let that distasteful decision settle within her.

"How do we beat her, though?" Nica persisted.

"I could distract her long enough to get Hafgufa to release Emily, and then all of us can get away as fast as we can." Holding Jimi's gaze, she asked, "Do you think you can let slip to the house that I'm here? Alone?"

"The house is bad. I don't trust it not to blab about me. But I could ask something else here that isn't as awful feeling." He glanced around. "That carpet."

Jimi placed a hand on the landing's carpet, a brown patterned wool rug. He mentally conversed for a moment and then turned to her. "The carpet says she's not a demon. That might be why she felt friendly. She says she's a gnome and her name's Lemon Lyda. She's been here for years stuck as a rug because Tuuli thought she was a terrible guard of her treasures."

"What treasures?" Nica asked.

"The kids," Jimi said. "Tuuli sells them to her friends as servants. Except Lemon Lyda kept letting Tuuli's special kids escape. She says if we agree to free her, she'll let the house know that you're up here, but not mention me."

"Excellent," Abbie said, stunned at that flow of fascinating information, and more than willing to bargain. "If I transform her, she'll need to see you and me, Jimi, so we don't alarm her."

Abbie asked Ruth to take the invisibility spell off the two of them, leaving Nica and Eli still invisible. Once that was done, she used her cord to speak to the gnome, intending to release it, but then had a better idea.

Taking a page from her earlier success with Tuuli's gown, she suggested to Lemon Lyda that she might only be a prisoner as long as she believed she was one.

Lemon Lyda laughed and scoffed at Abbie for offering such a far-fetched idea.

"Try it," Abbie persisted. "Pretend you're normal again. Picture yourself in your mind as clearly as you can."

They all waited and the rug merely lay on the floor, unmoving. Disappointed, Abbie was about to use her cord to free her when the carpet began to wiggle and shake.

Eli hovered higher to protect Abbie and the kids. Just in time, too, because in a moment, the carpet vanished to be replaced by a light brown-skinned, tiny but pudgy woman.

Lemon Lyda stood about a hand span in height with a pointed nose and ears. Her patterned dress was in shades of green and brown, and she wore sturdy brown boots, with a kerchief tied over her head.

"Thanking you, missus," the gnome said with a solemn face, and curtsied. "Wish I'd known this trick decades ago. I'll pass on your message to the house."

"Give us a few minutes before you do that," Abbie said.

Lemon Lyda agreed and ran off into the shadows.

The surprising success of Lemon Lyda's transformation delighted Abbie because this might be exactly how she could free Emily, too. "If we can get Emily to free herself, it would be quicker than my cord dismantling the spell. And time is of the essence. Now, for the distractions. We have several tools."

"Like what?" Jimi asked.

"One I have in mind involves you, Jimi." She then laid out her idea of how to divert Tuuli during Emily's release. "Do you think you could pull that off?"

He closed his eyes, and when he opened them, he nodded with confidence. "Yup, I can do it."

"Excellent. But for this to work, Nica," Abbie gently warned the young girl, "you'll have to let go of your brother."

Nica had done an admirable job of protecting him so far, but she had to trust him now, as Abbie had learned to, by letting him act on his own. Nica hesitated, opposing emotions of hope and fear warring on her beautiful little face. "I can't lose him, too," she finally said in a soft voice.

"You won't," Jimi replied. "I'll be inside Eli the whole time, and Arthur's protection is over all of us."

Nica's lips were trembling as she stared at her younger brother, then slowly, she let go of his hand.

Both Abbie and Jimi hugged her in gratitude.

Abbie then roped in her next conspirator. "Hafgufa, can you convince Emily she's capable of releasing herself?"

"I can try," her cord said.

Abbie finally placed her hand on her circle. "Eli, the moment Emily is within you, don't wait for my order. Whisk all of us away from here as fast as you can. Head out of this underworld compound, and into the market, but travel in that random zig-zag pattern you did before. Got it?"

"Yes," Eli responded.

Abbie tapped her mirror. "Ruth, make Jimi invisible again."

She checked their reflections in the mirror to verify. Abbie was the only one visible. Satisfied, she asked Eli to hurry them downstairs to the third floor.

Abbie and her kids arrived on that landing to a scream of outrage erupting down the corridor. Lemon Lyda must have passed on her message to the house, which would have notified Tuuli. A door flung open and Tuuli rushed out, searching up and down the corridor.

Circles couldn't work outside the marketplace–all except for Eli. She wanted to keep that extraordinary feat a secret. She casually strolled toward Tuuli, being careful to remain within her invisible circle. Eli slide along the floor to keep pace around Abbie and brought along her kids. Hopefully, her feet were close enough to the floor for her to pull off this visual trick of the eye.

To Tuuli, it should look as if Abbie approached of her own volition, like anyone else outside the market environs, where circles no longer worked.

"Evening, Tuuli," Abbie said in a calm tone. "Sorry to arrive uninvited," she added as she drew closer. She wanted to keep Tuuli's attention on her face and not around her feet, which weren't quite touching the floor. "I'm searching for someone I need to return to her family."

"You're in my brother's domain now, Grimm," Tuuli said, "so you're in no position to request anything. You should have left when I gave you the chance."

That sounded ominous. Tuuli may not be a goddess, but she was a fae companion with powerful magic at her disposal. She could certainly do more damage to them than they could do to her. In rescuing Oliver, she and Nica had used up what little magical power they absorbed from Judith and Talin.

Abbie sensed she had a smidge of Judith's magic left, but planned to save that for the right moment. As for her Grimm weaponry, Arthur and Hafgufa were more aligned toward defense, not offense.

Best if they rescued Emily and got out of here as fast as they could. If they could.

Abbie needed to get closer to the open doorway of the room Tuuli vacated, so her cord could easily reach Emily. That required getting into a conversation.

"First, I'd like to apologize," she said to the fae companion. "I was bluffing about your clothing back in the market center. I didn't think that gown would listen to me."

Abbie spoke sincerely since she had never meant to humiliate Tuuli. Reminding this fae companion of that incident, however, made for a good first volley at her distraction campaign. "For that offense, I'm truly sorry."

A blush spread up Tuuli's neck and face, leaving her quite beautiful, if furious. "Why haven't you left the market? I heard you found the children you sought."

"I did," Abbie said. She was almost at the doorway, less than two meters away from Tuuli. "Thank you for asking after them. They're safe and on their way home. I stayed to find another child I met from here. Her name is Emily."

Chapter Sixteen

Abbie stopped when she was within touching distance of her opponent, and right beside the open doorway. She held her hand up beside her waist. "The child I seek stands this tall. Quite sweet. A fellow named Zander kidnapped her when she was a little and has been using her to trap other magical kids."

"Zander is no longer a problem," Tuuli said, waving an arm in dismissal. "His child-acquiring scheme has ended. You no longer need to worry on that score."

"Good to hear." Abbie sent Hafgufa down the back of her leg and slithering across the floor into the room. "Do you miss your circle when outside the market? They are ingenious devices. Since using one, I find walking quite tedious."

"But necessary." Tuuli moved around Abbie. She paced back and forth in front of the parlor's doorway where Emily was kept. "Those circles are a visitor's only reliable protection. Something you've now lost by stepping outside the market."

Time for distraction number two. When Tuuli's pacing put her the furthest distance from the room, Abbie seized her opportunity and placed the one Taoist spell she knew on her enemy's feet.

She rooted Tuuli to a spot where her sight into the room was impeded. As she finished casting that spell, she realized she'd used up the last of Judith's borrowed magic. She was on her own now.

Her opponent came to an abrupt halt and glanced down at her bare feet in confusion. "What have you done?"

"Much better to converse while standing still, don't you think?" Abbie asked.

"Release me this instant!"

Tuuli grunted and flailed, trying to release herself. Beside Abbie, Jimi, invisible to Tuuli, hurried over to the edge of Abbie's circle facing the room. She silently instructed Eli to stretch into the room, allowing the boy to still stay within the circle's protection, but go to where Emily was located.

Nica's hand gripped Abbie's shirt in fear as her brother moved away from them. Though he was invisible, he waited until he was out of line of sight from Tuuli before he used his Yousef-borrowed magic to change his form.

The young Indian boy in blue jeans, a white shirt, and trainers then transformed into a skinny Caucasian brown-haired girl. She wore a too-large and frayed, green polka-dot dress, with scuffed Mary Janes on her feet.

He'd even matched Emily's taller height. Clever boy.

"Hafgufa," Abbie called mentally. *"How's it going?"*

"Emily has freed herself."

Excellent. Abbie retracted her cord into her arm as the real Emily toward Jimi. Abbie tapped her mirror and ordered Ruth to make Jimi visible.

Distraction number three coming up.

The two children stood, like a pair of identical twins, one behind the other. When they moved, Eli shrank back toward Abbie, matching Jimi's steps. The real Emily appeared stunned, her gaze trained on Abbie, while the fake Jimi-Emily enjoyed herself way too much as she stared at Tuuli.

"No!" Tuuli shouted when she glanced up and spotted the two children. "That's impossible."

The fake Emily took the real Emily's hand and pulled her inside Eli.

Tuuli, still rooted to where she stood, swung her frantic gaze from one child to the other in confusion as she tried to figure out who was the real Emily. "How did you duplicate that child? She's mine. You can't have her."

The moment Emily was safely within the circle, Eli whizzed them down the corridor, Tuuli's screams of rage echoing behind them. The circle left the house and zigged and zagged around the underworld compound, moving ever closer to the market.

Abbie sensed the moment the fae companion broke free of the "Don't move" spell. It was like the sting of a stretched elastic band striking back once snapped.

Soon, they entered the market, but Tuuli was nowhere in sight. Had they lost her? Now she was free, why wasn't she following Abbie? Or did it take her longer to travel without a circle? Abbie hoped so. They passed the celestial section, and the watery one. Finally, Eli sped into the market and then toward the entrance with the Griffin statues standing guard.

Abbie spotted Tuuli then, in her light magic form, fiery sparks flicking everywhere in fury. She'd arrived here ahead of them, waiting to ambush Abbie and the kids.

"Eli, stop!" Abbie cried out in panic.

He halted abruptly just outside the market entrance, jarring them. Straight ahead stood Tuuli, between them and the car park.

All those nearby ran for cover back into the market. Even the guard, Carlos, hid behind one of the giant griffin pedestals.

"You left my protected underworld home so fast," Tuuli's

words thundered in the air for all to hear. "I'd like to know how. Is that also how you arrived here so quickly? What artifact are you using for these feats? How many magical tools do you possess?"

Abbie cringed at her questions. Now everyone within hearing distance in the market would know about her Grimm artifacts, with the news spreading from there.

"I have such tools," she said in a bald lie. "I used a borrowed spell to take me out of the underworld compound. Then, once we returned to the marketplace grounds, I picked up my circle where I'd parked it."

Tuuli considered her words and then said, "Clever. Zander mentioned that you could make your circle invisible. But invisible or not, circles don't work outside the marketplace," she said with contempt. She raised her arm and a vibrating barrier appeared behind her. "See that? No spell will take you past that barricade to the car park. It's reinforced. The Spell Gate gatekeeper cannot help you get back to Earth. Now, you're mine to do with as I please."

Ah, that's why she waited out here for them, past this entryway into the market. She thought Abbie's circle would die once she left the market, leaving her powerless to escape. As a precaution, Tuuli had also created a fence between herself and the car park. Had she strengthened it enough to prevent Eli from traveling through it? Possible. One way to find out.

"You've lost this battle, Tuuli," Abbie said, shifting the children behind her in preparation to leave. "Give up gracefully and allow us to go home in peace."

"You've made a laughingstock of me, Grimm. And you can't have my compulsion spell-maker. She's too powerful a weapon."

"You can't have Emily," Abbie said flatly, aghast that anyone could think of a child as simply a weapon instead of a person with rights. "*Eli, see if you can zip around her...*"

Tuuli's light form spun, slowly at first, and then faster and faster. "If I can't have her, then no one will."

"Eli and Arthur," Abbie shouted, realizing they were past running away. If the barrier didn't stop them, Tulli's flaring magic would. "Get ready. She's going to strike."

She'd barely finished speaking when a spear of light shot out of Tuuli.

Abbie swung around and embraced the children in a protective hold. Eli's shield flared brighter than the sun, while Arthur's shield cupped them in a frizz of energy. Eli's blaring light heated, and even past Arthur's shield, he was scorching.

Then a scream of anguish reverberated across the air and went on and on. Abbie's ears rang painfully until she prayed for it to please stop.

All grew quiet then and the surrounding lights dimmed, no longer so harsh that it forced her to keep her lids closed. Finally, deeming it safe to open her eyes, she blinked and looked around to discover that this world had grown as dim as the underworld compound.

A swift glance confirmed the griffin statues still stood guard. That meant they hadn't been transported back to the demon compound.

She slowly straightened, searching for Tuuli. There, further out than where Abbie had last seen her. A form was lying on the ground. No longer spitting sparks, she was in her humanoid form, completely naked and unnaturally still.

Worried she was about to humiliate this woman again, Abbie told Eli to take her to Tuuli's side.

Her circle remained in place, faded and motionless. Had defending them depleted his strength?

Her EMT instincts kicked into gear because Tuuli wasn't moving, either. She'd have to check on Eli later.

"Arthur, are you well enough to keep your shield over the kids and me?"

"Yes," he responded, sounding strong.

Good. "I need to check on Tuuli," she said to the kids.

"Can't Eli take us over there?" Jimi asked, reverting to his normal form from looking like Emily's double.

"He's not responding." She hesitated a moment, and then asked, "I need you to guard each other while I'm away. Can you do that?" She trusted her kids could take care of themselves. They were quite remarkable.

All three children nodded, and Abbie left Eli to hurry toward her immediate concern. The supine Tuuli.

"Be careful!" Nica shouted after her.

Abbie arrived at the fae companion's side and quickly checked for vitals. It took a moment, but finally, she felt the faint *thud, thud* of a weak pulse. Abbie released a huff of relief. Tuuli was also breathing. It was slow and shallow, but present. She was alive, if wasted, in so many worrisome ways. Her hair had gone completely silver, thinned, and bare in places.

Abbie laid her jacket over Tuuli's now elderly form. She gently tapped the woman's wrinkled cheek. "Wake up."

Tuuli remained unresponsive, needing more help than Abbie could provide. Leaving her lying on the ground, she ran back to the entrance and called out, "Carlos! I need you."

He ran up to her. "I saw it all, *señorita*. When Queen Tuuli struck at you, your circle appeared and sent her bolt straight back at her, only charged a hundredfold stronger." He shook his head in wonder before looking over at the kids. "Where is your other child?"

Abbie tapped her mirror twice, and Nica appeared beside Jimi, eliciting a squeal of surprise from Emily.

"Carlos," Abbie said to regain his astonished attention, before telling him what she'd found after examining Tuuli.

"Her magic *es desaparecido*," he said, glancing over at the fae companion. "There's no aura of power around her. And if what you say about her aging is true... I'd say she's no longer immortal."

"She's going to need help when she awakens, Carlos," Abbie said. "Can you find someone from the fae compound to take care of her?"

"*Sí*," he nodded. "I put out the word, but she has few friends in the market, *señorita*." He patted Abbie's shoulder. "Never fear. I'll find someone trustworthy and compassionate."

Relieved about that, Abbie hurried over to kneel and place her hand over Eli. She felt nothing, no vibration or sense of his presence. "Jimi, see if you can reach him."

He placed his hand on the dim white circle. Then he looked up and shook his head, tears in his eyes.

"Oh, no," Nica cried out. "Abbie, I don't have any of Talin's magic left to help Eli."

From the corner of her eye, Abbie sensed the angel's presence. Without looking, she begged, "Can you save Eli?"

"He has fulfilled his mission," the angel replied.

Abbie's heart ached at the finality of that statement.

Then the angel added, *"As have you, Grimm Guardian,"* before she left.

"Wait," Abbie called out, swinging around to where the angel had been. "Surely there's something you can do for Eli? Please?"

"Who is she talking to?" Jimi whispered to his sister.

"The angel," Emily answered. "She spoke to it before."

Receiving no signs that the angel heard her plea or was even here any longer, Abbie sighed in deep disappointment. She touched the faded circle and whispered, "I'm so sorry, Eli. Thank you for all you did for us."

People exited the market then, slowly, cautiously. Giving Abbie and her kids a wide berth, they headed toward Tuuli.

"Abbie," Nica said. "These people don't look friendly. I think they might hurt Tuuli. We have to protect her."

"The griffins say these people hate Tuuli," Jimi confirmed.

Abbie nodded, seeing the worry in her children's gazes. They wanted to protect Tuuli. It warmed her heart to know how compassionate they were. And she was long done not listening to her kids. She stood and hurried the three kids over to the unconscious woman. Not waiting for instruction from Abbie, both Jimi and Nica spread out to keep everyone back. Emily, watching what they did, mimicked their gesture, spreading her arms wide to keep the crowd back.

"She's under our protection," Abbie said in a stern voice. "Stay back."

The folks, some human, some in flowing water form, one that looked like a moon, all obeyed her command and retreated, but they didn't leave.

Soon, Carlos returned with three folks. All three had

pointed ears and stood at least a head above even Abbie's tall frame. They wrapped Tuuli up in sackcloth and carried her into the market.

"*Vamoose*. Go on with all of you," Carlos shouted, gesturing for the crowd to disperse. "*Nada* left to see."

Once the crowd dispersed, he returned to Abbie's side and handed her jacket to her.

She took it, thanking him with deep gratitude. It was one of her favorites. Abbie shrugged into the black leather jacket, her hand automatically going to her pocket.

Thank heavens Ruth was still there. She'd forgotten to take out the mirror before covering Tuuli. Losing that artifact would have devastated her. Every one of her Grimm gifts meant the world to Abbie.

She sighed in relief that they'd all come out of this adventure unscathed. Not so Tuuli, her cohorts, or the market. "Carlos, what's happened to your sky? Why is it so dark?"

He glanced up before he responded. "After your invisible circle struck Tuuli, shock waves reverberated across the entire market. The barriers that sustain the market are only slowly recovering from those blasts." His quizzical glance met hers. "Guess that prophecy came true. The gatekeeper is working on restoring the market to its usual state."

"Do you think it can spare the time to send us home? We could take Zander's car over there."

Ortiz nodded. "I'll let it know you're ready to leave. We should have detached from Earth a while ago, but since you were still here, the gatekeeper delayed that schedule. It's been waiting for this call. Just think of it and it'll come for you."

She couldn't believe her presence had so affected the

market's smooth operation. "Thank you for all your help. Your wish stones saved a fae tree's life."

He started at her words, and then nodded, pleased.

She returned to Eli to find he had shrunk to a tiny, faded circle.

"Can we take him with us, Abbie?" Jimi asked, picking up Eli.

Abbie nodded. They might have lost the last of their friends' borrowed magic, but Judith or Talin could help Eli.

When the four of them reached the black hatchback, she noticed Zander had carelessly left it unlocked. Brilliant. Abbie sent Zander's spirit a silent thank you.

Jimi and Emily got into the back seat, while Nica took the front seat. Abbie sat in the driver's seat and shut her eyes. The moment she thought of the gatekeeper, claws appeared to grab the hatchback.

"Hang on!" she warned the kids.

When the gatekeeper deposited them back in the Sevenoaks shopping center's car park, she breathed a sigh of relief.

Then Jimi cried out, "Eli didn't come with us."

She swallowed this latest letdown, but wasn't about to argue with the gatekeeper. Who knew, Eli might have vanished completely by the time of transport. At least she and the children had returned home safely. She settled for that huge blessing.

The Kent sky was pitch black. It must still be nighttime here, even though it had felt as if they'd spent a day or more in the market. A lone lampstand nearby helped them see each other.

Abbie checked the ignition and the sun visor, but found no keys. She could use Hafgufa or...

"Jimi," she said, "could you get the car to start for us?"

He nodded, but as they waited, the car remained silent.

"What's wrong?" she asked, glancing back.

Jimi shrugged. "The car says you're not the owner. So, shove off."

"How are we going to get home?" Nica asked.

Not in the mood to fight with the car, Abbie got out, and the kids followed her.

She instead used her cord to contact Talin and Judith to let them know she and the kids were back and needed a lift. "There are four of us," she warned her friends. "Emily is with us. We'll need to take her back to her mum before heading to St. Michael's."

"Oh," Emily said, looking less than thrilled by that plan. "I couldn't believe it when I saw you outside that room in Tuuli's house," the child said. "That you came looking for me."

"A promise is a promise," Abbie replied with a reassuring smile, wondering where this was leading.

Emily came closer and tentatively asked, "Would you all be very mad if I said I'd rather go home with you instead of to my mum's?"

"I don't mind," Jimi said. "You can sleep on the sofa. Judith does that sometimes."

"Sure," Nica said. "You can be our sister." She turned to Abbie. "Can she?"

"That's one option," Abbie said, studying Emily and wondering at her hesitancy to reunite with her mother. "But why don't you want to see your mother, Emily?"

The child shrugged. A careless gesture. "She's probably forgotten all about me by now."

"If you were my child," Abbie said, "I wouldn't forget you. Ever."

"You're not her." Emily glanced up into Abbie's eyes and asked, "Don't you want me?"

Abbie opened her arms and Emily rushed in. She held her close for a precious moment, her gaze falling on the other two children who inched closer to get in on the hug, too.

They were still standing like that when a police unit pulled up beside them, lights flashing.

Talin rushed out with Judith right at his heels. They'd driven together, which made Abbie wonder why they hadn't brought two cars. Now they'd have too many piling into that one police unit.

"Oh, thank heavens, you're all safe," Talin said.

"We thought we'd lost the three of you," Judith said, "and instead, it looks like we gained one."

Abbie introduced Emily. "She thinks her mother's forgotten her."

"Far from the truth," Talin replied. "We located your mum, Emily. Ever since you were taken, she's been anxiously searching for you. While on our way here, we notified her you were back safe and sound."

"Oh, no," Emily said, tears in her eyes. "When she finds out what I've done, she won't like me."

Judith knelt to speak to the child. "Emily, not only does your mother know the horrors of what you've lived with, she's heartbroken that she couldn't protect you from that harm."

Just then, another car pulled up beside them, and a woman

with red hair rushed out. She hesitated as she laid eyes on all of them crowded together. Slowly, everyone moved apart to reveal Abbie standing alone, holding Emily's hand.

Emily inched closer to Abbie and hid her face.

Seeing the sorrow in the mother's eyes, Abbie took a full breath and sang. "Baa, baa, black sheep, have you any wool?" She paused and raised an eyebrow at the mother.

The woman's eyes widened and then she sang brokenly, "Yes, sir, yes, sir, three bags full."

"One for the master, and one for the dame," Abbie continued.

"And one for the little boy," Emily's mother sang.

"Who lives down the lane," Emily finished and ran into her mother's open arms, bawling, "Mama."

"Oh, my baby," her mother hugged Emily. Over her child's shoulder, she mouthed, *"Thank you,"* to Abbie.

• • • •

"IS ROBERT ALL RIGHT?" was Abbie's first question as Talin and Judith drove them all home.

"Gran says he's recovering," Judith replied from the driver's seat. "Slowly. Despite that, he's the one who insisted we take part in that fist bump when we felt you three start it. Since we could touch each other during those times, he wanted us to see if we could send you some of our energy through the link. Did that work?"

"Yes," Nica said, "I got your powers, Talin."

"I got Yousef's," Jimi said. "I could change into anything I wanted, even into Emily, to fool Tuuli."

Talin glanced over his shoulder from the front passenger

seat to meet Abbie's gaze. His frown spoke of confusion. "Yousef's only ever changed into a Siamese or that Bengal tiger. Does this mean he can do more than he believes?"

Abbie nodded, but wasn't certain Yousef would be keen to hear this news. He wanted to be rid of his powers, not expand them. Putting off that conversation, she said, "I received your power, Judith. That helped us save a fae tree and escape from Tuuli."

"And Robert's ability helped Eli travel through walls," Nica added.

"Who's Eli?" Judith asked.

"Our travel circle," Jimi said. "He died." Some of his cheer dimmed, and he slumped into his seat beside Abbie.

Missing Eli, too, she kissed his head in sympathy. Before going to sleep tonight, she planned to send up a prayer for that circle.

"We'll have to hold another SB meeting," Talin said, "so you can fill in all the details."

"After Robert's recovered," Abbie agreed.

"Oh, I will meet Emily and her mother tomorrow," Talin said, "to help them both release their years-long trauma."

"Thank you!" Abbie said, that last worry dissipating.

"Callum and your parents have been asking after you," Judith said. "You'll have to reassure them once home."

She nodded, pleased to have such ordinary daily life matters to deal with instead of life and death issues.

"Abbie!" Nica sat up, looking startled. She leaned over to glance at her past her brother.

"Yes, Nica," Abbie said. "I know what you're about to ask. Consequences. The 'no jam' and 'no cleaning' for a month decree starts tomorrow. Any objections?"

"Aw, Abbie," Jimi sulked.

"Abbie!" Nica said again.

"What's the matter?" Abbie asked, her concern now shooting up to match the anxiety in Nica's gaze.

"Goddess Kali is calling. She says she's been looking for me and we need to talk."

"About what?" Abbie asked, but Nica had vanished.

THE END

• • • •

CRAVE MORE OF THE STANDARD Bearers' adventures? In Book 6, **Death is Uncovered**[1], Abbie discovers that someone is after her Grimm artifacts, and she will do anything to keep them safe.

• • • •

IF YOU ENJOYED THIS story, please consider leaving a brief review for this book wherever you purchased it. The review will help other readers decide if they'd enjoy reading it, too.

• • • •

SIGN UP FOR SHEREEN'S Newsletter to learn about her new releases.

http://www.subscribepage.com/c9u7e6

Thank you for reading!

---

1. https://books2read.com/DIUBook6

Don't miss out!

Visit the website below and you can sign up to receive emails whenever Shereen Vedam publishes a new book. There's no charge and no obligation.

https://books2read.com/r/B-A-POZG-WDZBC

BOOKS 2 READ

Connecting independent readers to independent writers.

Did you love *Death Comes Up Short*? Then you should read *Death is Uncovered*[2] by Shereen Vedam!

[3]

A frantic search. A powerful opponent. A hard choice.

EMT Abbie Grimshaw accepts that danger is a part of her life, but this time, the danger isn't to her.

It's to her two kids. One gets kidnapped.

The clues lead Abbie and her friends to an informant specializing in magical artifacts and the discovery that the villain may be after Abbie's Grimm artifacts.

These powerful items are the world's best defense against dark forces. But can Abbie sacrifice her kid's life for the chance

---

2. https://books2read.com/u/mgN5yv

3. https://books2read.com/u/mgN5yv

to save the world?

If you enjoy magical thrillers with a fairy tale flavor, you'll love discovering this new face on the Grimm scene.

Pick up this magical adventurous mystery today!

Read more at www.shereenvedam.com.

Also by Shereen Vedam

Harrington Bay Mystery

Sage It Out

Missing You

Outside the Circle Mystery

To Capture Love

Death Takes a Detour

Death Shifts Gears

Death Smells Disaster

Death Swipes Right

Death Comes Up Short

Death is Uncovered

Death is Delayed

Death is Unleashed

Outside the Circle Mystery Boxed Sets and Bundles

Outside the Circle Mystery: Boxed Set Books 1-3

Tales of Ryca

Hidden

Hushed

The Cauldron Effect

Coven at Callington

Warlock from Wales

Love Spell in London

Standalone

Tales of Ryca: The Complete Series

Torn

The Cauldron Effect: The Complete Series

Believe

Innocent

Watch for more at www.shereenvedam.com.

About the Author

Once upon a time, USA Today bestselling author Shereen Vedam read fantasy and romance novels to entertain herself. Now she writes heartwarming tales braided with threads of magic and love and mystery elements woven in for good measure.

Shereen's a fan of resourceful women, intriguing men, and happily-ever-after endings. If her stories whisk you away to a different realm for a few hours, then Shereen will have achieved one of her life goals.

Please consider leaving a review wherever you purchased this book.

Read more at www.shereenvedam.com.

www.ingramcontent.com/pod-product-compliance
Lightning Source LLC
Chambersburg PA
CBHW070349200726
48294CB00003B/812
9781989036198